Psyche

Psyche

PETER
MICHALOS

NAN A. TALESE
DOUBLEDAY
New York   London   Toronto   Sydney   Auckland

🌱

PUBLISHED BY
NAN A. TALESE
an imprint of Doubleday, a division of
Bantam Doubleday Dell
Publishing Group, Inc.
1540 Broadway
New York, New York 10036

DOUBLEDAY and the portrayal of an anchor
with a dolphin are trademarks of Doubleday,
a division of Bantam Doubleday Dell
Publishing Group, Inc.

This novel is a work of historical fiction.
Names, characters, places, and incidents
relating to nonhistorical figures are either the
product of the author's imagination or are
used fictitiously. Any resemblance of such
nonhistorical incidents, places, or figures to
actual events or locales or persons, living or
dead, is entirely coincidental.

Book design by Marysarah Quinn

Library of Congress
Cataloging-in-Publication Data
Michalos, Peter
Psyche / Peter Michalos. — 1st ed.
p.   cm.
1. Freud, Sigmund, 1856–1939—Fiction.
2. Schliemann, Sophia Kastromenos
—Fiction.   I. Title.
PS3563.I3312P78   1993
813'.54—dc20   92-44236
                                      CIP

ISBN 0-385-42405-1
Copyright © 1993 by Peter Michalos
All Rights Reserved
Printed in the United States of America
August 1993

1   3   5   7   9   10   8   6   4   2

First Edition

To Kathleen Hale

"I have just carried out one resolution which one group of people, as yet unborn and fated to misfortune, will feel acutely. Since you can't guess whom I mean I will tell you: they are my biographers. I have destroyed all my diaries of the past fourteen years, with letters, scientific notes and the manuscripts of my publications."

—*Sigmund Freud to his betrothed,*
28 April 1885

PREFATORY
REMARKS

20 Maresfield Gardens, London
6 September 1939

I suppose a man who has been the indisputable favorite of his mother keeps for life the feeling of a conqueror. Even today, at the height of my fame, I am not really a man of science—not a thinker, not an experimenter, not even an observer. I am nothing but by temperament a *conquistador*—an adventurer, if you want to translate the word—with the curiosity, boldness, and tenacity that belong to that type of being.

I wanted to be Hannibal, I wanted severed Roman genitals festooned around my neck. I never wanted to be a doctor! Medicine and sick people disgusted me. I was fascinated by the past, by Plato's theory of reminiscence, the whole idea of eternal return. I cared nothing about the future (to average bourgeois common sense I was lost long ago) and never believed in it. The years beyond were hidden from me as though by a screen. But I possessed the excellent quality of being able to believe in my own judgment. I knew I had to do the thing that was right for my nature.

As a result I did a number of things that any sensible person would be bound to consider very rash. Especially in my youth. People have always seen something alien in me, and the reason for this is that in my youth I was never young. I was always experimenting, always sublimating. I felt as though I had inherited all the defiance and all the passions of my ancestors and would gladly sacrifice my life for one great moment in history. But at the same time I felt helpless and incapable of expressing my ardent passions, even by a word or a poem. So I restrained myself, always, and it is this restraint, this terrible restraint, that people sense in me and that frightens them.

I had one important hobby, my passion for antiquities. The busts of goddesses were my only real extravagance. In 1886, to supplement my income from lecturing at the university, I opened a neurological practice and became involved in other people's lives. Slowly, inexorably, the terrible secrets of the family became my special province. I had newly answered the question of marriage. Just thirty years old, a former pupil of Charcot in Paris, I stood for an incomparably freer sexual life than society was willing to permit. Inevitably I made mistakes (the most revealing you can imagine), mostly with female hysterics.

Fortunately, the truth is fragile. There is nothing known that cannot become unknown, nothing found that cannot become lost. Twice before I have destroyed my words. All my old friendships and associations passed again before my eyes and mutely met their doom. Poems, notes, diaries, manuscripts— the fire cleansed them. But now the fire is within. I am dying, with little to fear from the scrabble of pencils. Let my biographers file what follows under Freud the son or Freud the father, the erotic or the neurotic Freud; let them scratch their heads, and chafe, and go astray. My science of the psyche, my beautiful psychoanalysis, is alive. The sexual theory is triumphant, America penetrated, the succession provided for. It is time to give Lucy/Atalanta her due, even if the *goyim* hold it against me.

I have written about her elsewhere, but in terms that were deliberately vague. It was a magnificent case: race memories, infantile seduction, visual and auditory disturbances—everything one could hope for. The girl was unusually intelligent and creative. It was she who was the explorer, the archaeologist; I was merely her compass, her instrument. Through me she reinvented the ancient science of hypnotism. Through me she created the therapy—the only therapy—that entirely suited her.

Effortlessly combining the girlish and the heroic, she was from the best society. Her culture was unrivaled, she had every talent. In addition, she was beautiful, with hair of wild gold. Her eyes were the color of trees, constantly changing in the light but always deep, making you feel as if she saw into your thoughts. She was intoxicating, pulling together forces from every side—forces that could crush. There was enormous power in her, all the mythopoeic forces of mankind. She possessed a tremendous unconscious fantasy system, which I had to drag into the light of day with unspeakable effort and patience, but on days when I didn't see her I felt short of a drug. Was she a penance to expiate for my indifference to women in my youth?

Her illness formed the boundary between the two phases of her sexual life, of which the first was masculine in character and the second feminine. Having known the freedom of a boy, she tried again and again to deny the humiliating feminine role forced upon her. Having experienced boyish traits and inclinations throughout girlhood, she became profoundly hysterical at puberty. Unfortunately, her treatment was a failure. She acted out an essential part of her recollections and fantasies instead of reproducing them on the couch. She took her revenge on me as she wanted to take her revenge on her father; she deserted me as she believed herself to have been abused and deserted by him.

The father. Always the father. Herr O was a man of rather unusual activity and talents, a large manufacturer in very comfortable circumstances. His daughter was most tenderly attached to him; and for that reason her critical powers, which developed early, took all the more offense at many of his actions and peculiarities. Not to mince words, Herr O was a paranoid, with an imagination fatally seared by eroticism. Before he died he made me promise never to publish anything about his daughter's case while she remained alive. This verbal guarantee of secrecy has placed quite extraordinary restrictions upon my choice of material for over fifty years; I can allow it to do so no longer. I am a genius, after all, and this was the time when I lived at the height of my energy and my imagination, manufacturing eternity as well as emotion.

And there is another reason for publishing the case. It

documents for the first time the relationship between my occasional use of cocaine and the development of psychoanalysis. Perhaps I can be forgiven—*nicht wahr?*—my original rather touching faith in the "divine plant." You must remember there had never been a safe psychic stimulant in the history of the world before. I saw it as a magical substance, an instrument of almost unbelievable curative power. The use of drugs for euphoriant and psychedelic purposes had been recorded from the very beginnings of history; the Bible and the Greek and Roman heroic myths contain numerous references to psychotropic substances.

Of *course* coca is toxic; one has only to notice its stimulative effect on the genitalia to know it is a poison. But "everything is poison and nothing is poison," as Paracelsus observed. Cocaine was never meant to be inhaled, injected, abused. Taken orally, in the proper doses, it is capable of producing the most exalted mental feeling imaginable—far more ecstatic than anything experienced from the use of opium or alcohol. I remain an enthusiast and user to this day (very small doses against depression). What of it? How can there be a "bad" drug?

Unfortunately, the lion's share of coca credit went elsewhere—that fool Koller's use of the drug as a local anaesthetic produced a sensation. I was shattered (I admit it); I had missed world fame by a hair's-breadth. The appledrug was to be my second chance. Not that it matters: there is no judge between gods and men.

Here is what happened. Two days ago a certain Herr K, supposedly a reputable writer and art dealer from Berlin, came to see me with a document purporting to be the "Diary of Lucy O" for the years 1886–87. He placed the unbound, flaking yellow pages into my hands and named an exorbitant price; then, without warning, he began heaping the vilest, most filthy abuse on me, calling me a "monster" and a "child molester." I raised my arm to ring for Anna, to show him from the house, but against my will my eyes dropped . . .

. . . *dissolved, I have neither bulk nor weight. My heart comes undone and falls into my father's chest. I am no more than a mouth attached to his breast, a father spouse . . .*

I decided to pay what he asked.

The diary is authentic, a revelation. With a view to publication, I have been driven back to my old journal of the case, the original working record of Lucy's analysis, to postdate my entries and match them with hers. It breaks my heart to reveal who I was so many years ago, but as always the only possible decision has been to reprint my original text—this fragment of an analysis of a case of hysteria—without alteration from the notes I made in the evenings after the treatments. I was so young! I know now that when it is possible to work in the "friendlier" aspects at an early stage, the course of the analysis may be retarded and obscured, but the existence of the relationship is better guaranteed against sudden and overwhelming disturbances. After 1888, I scrupulously avoided the erotic potential of psychotherapy, its awful loverlike privacy and intimacy. Soon afterward I invented the transference as a kind of inhibition against at least the most obvious sexual temptations.

Before the case of Lucy O, I had only obscurely understood the newness and bizarreness of the psychoanalytic relationship, its utter unlikeness, in its opposites of love and hate, veiledness and nakedness, to life's other relationships. But I had learned that for sex to be kept at bay in therapy, one and only one member of the therapeutic pair—the doctor—has to behave himself. In not a few of my early cases, especially with women and where it was a case of elucidating erotic trains of thought, the patient's cooperation became a personal sacrifice that had to be compensated for by some substitute for love. Ineluctably, when I gave my female patients permission to declare their love for me, psychoanalysis proper was under way.

What else is there for me to say? I am well aware that there are many physicians (revolting though it may seem) who choose to read a history of this kind not as a contribution to the psychopathology of the neuroses but as a *roman à clef* designed for their private delectation. They will find little of sustenance here. Although the girl has become briefly famous, her personal circumstances must remain practically unknown to the international medical community. Who could possibly be aware that I was once her doctor? Of course, I cannot prevent the patient from being pained if her own case history should accidentally fall into her hands. But she will learn nothing from it she does not already know; and she may ask herself who besides her could discover from it that she is the subject—one of the subjects—of the Atalanta papers.

As for me, I no longer feel the need to suppress my personality. That need has been extinguished; I have succeeded where the paranoic fails. Let my Lucy speak; let her say that along with Oedipus and Electra, along with my theories of dreams and infant sexuality, Atalanta is the glory of my work. Who knows? This clumsy counterpoint of hers and mine may actually be the truth.

Prehistory

One

7 Rathausstrasse, Vienna

12 June 1886

During the past few weeks I've been experimenting with hypnosis (just with friends and family) and have achieved some small but noteworthy successes. Still, after the excitement of Paris, I feel isolated, scientifically dulled, lazy, resigned. I am *very* insufficiently occupied and correspondingly ill-humored. Really, it is too distressing for a medical man who spends every hour of the day struggling to gain an understanding of the neuroses not to know whether he is suffering from a logical or a hypochondriacal mild depression!

Martha was standing by the washbasin in my room at the hospital when I got back from Meynert's lecture. There was something strange about her; and for some reason she was wearing one of my white coats, much too big for her.

"Who let you in?" I tried not to sound too touchy and suspicious.

"The porter. We had a fascinating conversation."

"But we were supposed to meet in the courtyard."

"Yes, but you were supposed to arrive on time."

"You shouldn't enter a man's room, Martha. Not even if the man is your fiancé."

"Really?" With a coquettish expression of vexation she removed her white coat and hung it up. The dress underneath was elegant, albeit modest. "Do you prefer me like this?"

"My darling, my princess, my—"

I was on the verge of throwing myself on her when I noticed she was looking at me somewhat mistrustfully, so I drew away and said, "Are you angry with me?"

"Not if you love me, Sigmund."

"I love you more than anything."

"Do you think I'm beautiful?"

"Oh, Martha, I suppose you are not beautiful in a painter's or a sculptor's sense—you know I cannot flatter. But the magic of your being expresses itself in your countenance and your body . . . and don't forget, beauty only stays a few years and we have to spend a long life together . . ."

"Ha!" It was a violent laugh, full of irony. "You always have to find explanations for everything. At the same time you're just amusing yourself, so leave me in peace."

"But I can't stop wondering—"

"Don't put yourself forward so much, Sigmund. I don't want to be the wife of the eminent Dr. Freud. I'd much rather be the wife of a family doctor; I prefer them to specialists."

"Martha . . . did I ever tell you that when I was a boy I used to call the *goyim* Romans? We, the Jews, were Carthaginians; I was Hannibal, the great man of Carthage, sworn to wreak vengeance upon Rome. Well, the only way I can become Hannibal is by becoming the best doctor in Vienna!"

She looked at me, dumbfounded. "You never told me that."

"You know very well how hard I find it to talk about myself."

"Why are you like that?"

"I don't know. Poverty, perhaps. Or an excessively long engagement! Four and a quarter years! I swear to you, Martha, everything will change once we're married."

Later I thought, where is the playfulness of youth? I feel for Martha a "grand" passion that is gloomy, tense, ascetic, secretive.

21 June

Merck has sent me twenty grams of the little-known alkaloid cocaine, with a note asking me to study its physiological action. Could I please sample, test, etc., and report my findings as soon as possible? (I suppose it is an honor to be buttonholed by a captain of the chemical-pharmaceutical industry?)

Hurrah! This morning Breuer called me into his office, lighted my cigar, and gave me a patient, a girl of sixteen, Lucy O. He described her severe muscular contractions, convergent squint, and left-sided occipital headaches; then he hinted at something truly interesting, a case worth recording in some detail. "The etiology may be relevant to your sexual theory of hysteria, Sigi. This girl suffers from acute fright and zoöpsia. She sees animals that aren't there, creatures that cringe and bare their teeth at her. Yesterday, in the Ringstrasse, she saw a thin, vicious, overbred dog at my side, which growled when she tried to approach me."

"The parents?"

"Her mother died a year ago. Since then, daughter and father, a man in his late forties, have been traveling on the Continent to find the girl a husband. I wonder . . . Would you care to accompany me to their hotel?"

It was a beautiful expectant morning. Our horse pulled eagerly, foam flying from its mouth. As the elegant Bayrischer Hof swam into view, I looked at it admiringly, remarking the wrought iron railings and plumed helmets of the guards. My gaze rose up along the high walls, and for a moment I saw it as a fortress floating in the sky—gray, secluded, and armed— with the city's swift life rushing heedlessly underneath.

In the Os' suite my impression was of opulence and scented air, as if smoke were rising everywhere from large fires. The strange smoky yellow light was evidently caused by the high ornate amber and rose stained glass windows (surely an oddity in a hotel room?). Beneath them the father stood with a watchful impenitent awareness. Breuer projected me into the semidarkness: "Allow me to present my colleague, Dr. Sigmund Freud, who specializes in nervous disorders and mental illnesses."

The daughter padded forward soundlessly. She is a beautifully formed, very well-grown child, as white as milk and honey. She has a narrow head, masses of golden blond hair, and a tall figure with unformed breasts and slender arms. Although her face shows remarkable intelligence and exceptional sensitivity, the element of sexuality is astonishingly undeveloped in her. Even at a distance, something about her conveys a sense of boyishness and intense individual isolation. One infers intelligence from the enormous reserve that seems to veil her being, but clearly something formidable is happening to her. An intermittent physical restlessness is taking possession of her like a madness, twitching her limbs when she doesn't want to twitch them, jerking her spine upright when she doesn't want to jerk but prefers to rest comfortably.

"Do you think I look like my father?" she said. An infantile range of expressions formed on her face: a scowl, a challenge, a frown, a brief relaxation into languor, etc.

"Yes." I answered at random but with deliberate harshness. After all, she was deliberately trying to provoke me.

"That's just what you shouldn't have said. I don't look like him at all. Take a good look."

"I don't agree that you should tease our visitor, Lucy. Of course your eyes are not quite like mine. You have your mother's beautiful hazel eyes." Herr O was small, graceful, blue-eyed, and faintly monstrous. No one could have denied him the epithet of "handsome": black hair and beard; little red mouth with scornful pout; deep, resonant voice. I saw as well that he had an unusual talent for condescension: he could accurately weigh and measure out the exact quantity of affability required. "My daughter has perplexed several physicians before yourselves. I don't expect you to perform any miracles."

I said as smoothly as possible, "Dr. Breuer has told me something of your daughter's case. May I inquire as to what method of treatment she has been following?"

"I was told that mountain air—"

"Completely beside the point, I'm afraid. Fräulein O is suffering from hysteria. It is of course a psychosis."

"How dare—"

"On the contrary, hysteria is a perfectly respectable disease of the nervous system. Among hysterics are found people of the strongest will, the clearest intellect, the greatest character, and the highest critical power. The disease occurs with alarming frequency in the best families in Europe."

"And you treat this disease precisely how?"

"I employ a method that has only recently begun to be used in the positive sciences: induced somnambulism."

"Hypnosis? I must say, you surprise me, Dr. . . . . What did you say your name was?"

I had taken an enormous dislike to him and he to me. I could not endure him even in principle, simply as a form of existence, the O pattern. His combination of mind, business, good living, sensuality, and intelligence was something I found in the highest degree intolerable.

"Freud. Lecturer in neuropathology at the Pathological Institute. My clinical experiments suggest that hysterical people are particularly suggestible to stimuli. What is necessary is only to produce in them, by means of hypnotic suggestion, positive unconscious forces to neutralize the negative ones."

"But why has my daughter become sick?"

"Why? Do I know why my back aches? Do I even know why I smoke? I think I have an urge to do so, but what lies hidden behind my urge? What secret motive? What command? What lies hidden behind all our urges, all our fears? An invisible world. Forces. Our conscious motives are not the true ones."

I suggested that while Herr O considered the possible usefulness of hypnotic-suggestive therapy, Lucy should separate from him and go into a nursing home where I could see her every day. This both she and her father agreed to without raising the slightest objection.

⇥

Bayrischer Hof
2 July

I cannot sleep. I see my hand coming up to turn the page of my diary, choosing just the right moment to turn the page and drop into the future . . .

There must be a spirit that won't leave me alone. All my life it has been with me. I shall call it the Beast, though it is many beasts.

Last night, when I looked at myself in the mirror before going to bed, I was taken aback. That couldn't be me, that glistening gray face with the burning black eyes.

Suddenly all the lines in the room went crooked. Every-

thing became alien and terrifying. There was a powerful baleful wolf lurking there coldly in the depths. "What is it you want?"

"The great chill is coming."

I have met my "doctor." He is thirty—thick black beard, thick eyebrows. Fine eyes, dark and forbidding, sunk deep in their sockets.

His hands are well cared for.

He looks at me like a deer with his deer eyes.

Bellevue Sanatorium
8 July

Arrived last night in pouring rain . . . Father throwing money at the porters, everything rather damp . . . stupendous misty blue mountains in the distance.

The owner, Herr Binswanger, came out with an umbrella to say, "The Bellevue Sanatorium in Kreuzlingen is one of the best and most modern private sanatoria for nerve and mood illnesses. It is run strictly according to the principle of non-restraint, and great value is placed on the contact of the patient with healthy people, such as the family of the attending physician."

The doctors wear white coats . . . almost all have beards. In the hall, Frau Binswanger pressed me to her heart, kissed me, told me she liked me so much, I was such a good person. Do I deserve this? Can anyone really love me in this way? My room is spotless but not very homey: spare, simple furniture, tasteless yellow wallpaper. The window looks out on a little square courtyard.

Please, please. Don't let me suffer for no reason. Don't let some disease such as "nervousness" paralyze my mind and destroy my abilities.

Let me trust my doctors and nurses and no longer be so afraid of people. Let me think and speculate as little as possible. I shall attempt to leave myself entirely in the hands of divine might to see if I do not receive some sort of message. I remain hopeful, disregarding the anxiety that robs me of sleep and appetite and drives me crazily from place to place. I remain defiant because I have something noble and good to create. No pain is unbearable to me, no sacrifice too great, if only I can fulfill my sacred calling! I am no longer myself, no longer my wish, but unshakable, divine will! What do you wish, God? What have you decided in your councils, ye gods? Reveal to me your final purposes and may they be done!!

—+—

13 July

She started violently when I entered the room (I therefore arranged that the nurses and the house physicians, when they visit her, should give a loud knock at her door and not enter till she has told them to come in). Gone was the infanta of the Bayrischer Hof. Her face bore a strained and painful expression; her eyelids were drawn together and her eyes cast down.

She told me she has had fearful dreams: the legs and arms of chairs were all turned into snakes; a monster with a vulture's beak was eating at her all over her body; bears and other wild animals leapt upon her, and so forth. From time to time, perhaps in order to convince me of the vividness of her dreams and the genuineness of her afflictions, she raised her face to my own. At such moments her shining eyes held me with their look of glittering disorientation. She spoke in a low voice, as though with difficulty, but what she said was coherent and revealed an unusual degree of education and intelligence. This made it seem all the more strange when, every two or three minutes, she suddenly broke off, contorted her face into an expression of horror and disgust, stretched out her hands toward me, spreading and crooking the fingers, and exclaimed, in a changed voice, charged with anxiety, "Keep still! Don't say anything! Don't touch me!"

After each of these interpolations—apparently she was under the influence of some recurrent hallucination of a horrifying kind and was keeping the intruding material at bay with this formula—she took up what she had been saying without pursuing her momentary excitement any further, and without explaining or apologizing for her behavior (probably, therefore, without herself having noticed the interpolation). In reply to a question, she said she saw mice, rats, insects, snakes—her imagination seemed to select the classically loathsome creatures. One of her most persistent hallucinations is of a small, brightly patterned snake moving across the floor in the periphery of her vision. And her zoöpsia is accompanied by a terror of real animals. The mere touch of fur, even in a coat, causes her nausea.

I learned what follows of her circumstances. Her family came from central Germany, but had been settled for two generations in the Baltic provinces of Russia, where it possessed large estates. She was an only child of the tomboy type, generally quite active but occasionally troubled by inexplicable cravings for sleep. Lonely and intelligent, she embellished her life in a manner that probably influenced her decisively in the direction of her illness by indulging in systematic daydreaming. She described this as her "private theater." While everyone thought she was attending, she was actually living through "theatrical" experiences in her imagination; but she was always "on the spot" when she was spoken to, so that no one was ever aware of it.

Her mother had suffered from "waking daydreams," sleep-like states that occurred at odd times throughout the day, when she would literally fall asleep on her feet. There were also various afflictions of the eyes and ears, various disturbances of vision, and the like. For this reason, even as a child, Lucy had found herself drawn into especially intimate contact with her father, a vivacious man of the world who used to say that this daughter of his took the place of a son and friend with whom he could exchange thoughts. But Herr O regularly complained of his daughter's ambition, her moral sensibility, her giftedness, her excessive demand for love, the independence of her nature, which went so far beyond the feminine ideal, etc. He jokingly called her "cheeky" and "cocksure" and warned her against her habit of recklessly telling people the truth.

The patient is, in fact, greatly discontented with being a girl. She has no desire for a husband or children. She is full of ambitious plans. She wants to study and to have a musical training, she intends to learn additional languages, she is indignant at the idea of having to sacrifice her inclinations and her freedom of judgment to marriage. She nourishes herself on her family's prestige and social position, and she jealously guards everything that is bound up with these advantages. Three or four months ago, in Monte Carlo, her condition was temporarily improved by a course of electric baths. But once more, for several weeks, she has been very ill, with migraines, terrible depression, and insomnia alternating with drugged sleep.

I ordered her to be given electric baths, and I shall massage her whole body twice a day. She was not forbidden to see her father, to read, or to write letters.

—⊰⊱—

19 July

I want to try a new approach with my diary. I want to make a deliberate attempt to come to terms with my daily experience, to set things down clearly, in order . . . to pick out moments that have been particularly happy or sad and record them in words. Why not?

I feel I can even approach the subject of my dreams and my higher calling with calmness and deliberation. (Help me, diary. The thought that my higher calling might be only a ridiculous dream is insupportable. If all my intelligence and sensitivity have been granted only to help me perceive my uselessness for life! If I haven't the wits to discover something that I love more, that matters more, than myself!)

I remember one day (I could work it out to the very day it happened) I woke up out of the sleep of childhood. Immediately there was the conviction, all ready and waiting for me, that I had a call to bring something about, was chosen for some great purpose. I knew then that I would do something worth doing, and I ran for miles to improve my stamina, and I read every book I could get my hands on.

The question is, where does this need in me to believe in a higher calling come from? From my mother? She is dead, of course, her body in the earth and turned to dust; but I believe she was clairvoyant, she saw all time and space as one. Last night she appeared to me in a dream. She said I was learned in the old religious lore, I had come into the world to accomplish something great, I should just continue to live calmly and patiently and it would all come to pass.

But every day I feel more and more pressure on me. What is the pressure saying? What does it require of me? Is it divine in origin?

Why do I feel as though now, and only now, I am ready to begin?

(Am I raving? Is this insane nonsense?)

---

25 July

She complained of sleeplessness and storms in her head, of not being able to think, of being blind and deaf, of having two selves, a real one and an evil one that forced her to behave badly, and so on. I asked her to go behind the screen and remove her gown for the massage. She opened her mouth and exhaled, then sighed loudly before complying with my wishes in an exaggeratedly bored manner. I was to understand that she would cooperate, but only grudgingly. Her limit would be a kind of unwitting patient participation, like bringing urine to be analyzed or enduring the expression of pus.

Through heavy towels I massaged her lower back, buttocks, and thighs. She entertained me with gruesome stories of animals: how she had picked up a ball of white wool which turned into a mouse; how a bat had flown out of her wardrobe. Occasionally, as she spoke, she stared fixedly behind her and repeated her protective formula ("Keep still! Don't say anything! Don't touch me!").

"Are you seeing any animals now, fräulein?"

"No."

But her look of abstraction and rapt intensity inclined me to disbelief. I massaged the trapezius muscles down the back of her neck and along her shoulders. After a minute or two, she began to speak. She told me she experienced two entirely distinct states of consciousness, which alternated suddenly and without warning. In one of these states she recognized and "remained in" her surroundings; she was melancholy and anxious, but relatively normal. In the other state, her "second" consciousness, she hallucinated and experienced what she called "absences"—plastic scenes that swam before her eyes in their natural colors, with all the vividness of reality.

Apparently these scenes could be likened to a dream, especially in view of their colorful characters and plots, large gaps of memory, and continuous automatic associations. But lately the dreams were invading even her moments of clear consciousness, and she was losing all control of time. Against her will, she would start to hallucinate in the middle of a conversation and run off somewhere, perhaps start climbing a tree or something similar. If her interlocutor caught hold of her, she would quickly take up her interrupted sentence without knowing what had happened in the interval. But if, during the "second," something had been moved in the area, or someone had entered or left it, she would feel she had lost some time in her train of thoughts. Those around her would deny this and try to soothe her, but she would accuse them of doing things to her and leaving her in a muddle—even though at the same time as she was experiencing scenes with all the vividness of reality, she continued to experience her primary consciousness as well. She was very insistent upon this point. Even when she was in a bad condition (hallucinating ceaselessly for minutes at a time), a clear-sighted observer sat calmly in a corner of her mind, looking on at all the intensely interesting mad business with a clear, curious eye.

What am I to make of all this? Is her splitting of consciousness itself pathological, or are all of us potentially or actually hallucinating other people most of our lives? Is this even a fit question for a doctor (scientist) to ask?

And why is it that some of the case entries I write read like short stories? That, as one might say, they lack the serious stamp of science?

I suppose I should console myself with the reflection that the nature of the subject is evidently responsible for this, rather than any preference of my own. In studying hysteria, only a detailed description of mental processes really suffices—a description such as we are accustomed to finding in the works of imaginative writers.

Unfortunately, description is not therapy. What is my

method to be with her? Didactic-suggestive therapy? A combination of hypnosis, electricity, and talking?

Speak to Herr O re hypnosis—

30 July

That bit of cocaine I have taken seems to have worked wonders on my mood. My fatigue has miraculously disappeared. I feel as strong as a lion, gay and cheerful.

31 July

Herr O was so kind as to dine with me tonight at Café Griensteidl. Who is this man? Does it matter? Why do I feel a guttersnipe desire to throw stones or mud at him? Is it a specific detail of his physiognomy to which my distaste attaches itself, or simply the whole of it? His sexuality seems questionable to me, but I suppose some perverse trait or other is seldom absent from the sexual life of even normal people—?

He got quickly drunk (surely his indifference and contempt betray a consuming interest in my relationship with his daughter?). When I asked about Lucy's childhood, he slurred, "After lunch, I used to wrap her in velvet or brocade, with a long train, and put her on one of her horses." So much for the past.

As the evening wore on I made a too-passionate plea to be allowed to hypnotize his daughter. He looked at me for a moment with his brilliant paranoid intelligence as if I were quite mad; then he gave his consent. In retrospect, the only thing that surprised me was his asking me to obtain *her* permission as well. Is this Prussian guilt at work? Why should I have to drop everything and become a male nurse to a mental case and her obnoxious father? I see now that to take up science as a poverty-stricken man was madness! I must soon become a rich man, and then when they want something they will all have to come to me!

---

3 *August*

Something like magic is happening. I am seeing my father for the first time. We are trapped in a burning room. I hear the crackle of the flames, the screams of the victims. I feel the heat of the fire on my face . . .

5 *August*

The night is humid, warm. In the distance, plaintive notes of a violin float on the air. I feel so strongly my sense of déjà vu. I feel so strongly that I am the wild one, the one who walks among beasts and calms them, the one who is forever a maiden, never a man's woman, never a mother. Never! I could never surrender to a peaceful life in the bosom of my husband. Perfect stillness makes me anxious. No! I must always have people with passionate souls around me, I must be inspired by mighty and profound feelings, I must have music, art, literature, dancing. I was always the tireless one, ferocious, quick. I could always outrun all the boys I knew. I won races without trying most of the time—I always had more speed than I used. I could do handstands and somersaults and cartwheels perfectly, always, my knees perfectly straight, my toes pointed outward, my head tucked under, legs perfectly spinning, seven flips in one direction, seven in the other, hands positioned just so, head positioned just so, feverish, radiant with concentration, oblivious to everything . . .

6 August

    Keep still! Don't say anything! Don't touch me!

Two

Letter to Martha

10 August

Absolutely not! Princess! No last-minute postponements! I already miss you so much in every way! I suffer terribly from loneliness and longing because I have taken you to myself not just as sweetheart but as bride-to-be, comrade, and so forth! Therefore I live in the most painful privation! Martha! I do not enjoy anything at all! For weeks I haven't had a cheerful expression on my face.

Besides, I am reconciled to our being so poor. Why should my poverty be the one and only obstacle to our union? Why get so wrought up over a few shabby gulden? All we need is two or three little rooms where we can live and eat and receive a guest and a hearth where the fire for cooking does not go out. We shall be two together and far removed from the direst poverty, which doesn't prevent so many people from loving each other.

How long does one stay young, how long healthy? How long does one stay pliable enough to adapt oneself to the changing mood of the other? You would be an old maid if I let you wait until I can pay for everything, and you would have forgotten how to laugh.

15 August

"Good morning, fräulein."

"Good morning, Herr Doktor Freud."

"Let me come straight to the point, if you please. Your condition cannot be cured by massage and baths."

"I had never supposed that it could."

"With nervous disorders such as yours, purely symptomatic treatment therapy is a waste of time."

"You want to hypnotize me, don't you?" She spoke in a soft, childlike, venomous tone of voice.

"Hypnotic therapy could constitute a causal treatment of your illness, allowing us to approach the psychic events at its root. The main thing is not to expect a miracle cure; the treatment can last for months. Would you agree to undergo it?"

"You'll put me to sleep? And while I'm asleep you'll hammer Good into my head? I don't believe in that. Evil will swallow up Good. Don't you believe in Evil, Doctor?"

"Yes, I do."

"And in the Devil?"

"Fräulein, may I have your consent?"

"Yes, I suppose so, but I am not sure how it will turn out."

I took her by the arm and led her to the couch. As she sat down, I placed my right index finger along her nose between her eyes. "Look at my finger, Lucy. You will fall asleep. You are going to sleep. Sleep! You are sleeping. You are fast asleep."

I supported her, helping her to stretch out on the couch. Her eyes turned up, the whites showed, and she let herself fall back, her arms straight against her sides, her breathing even. Her skin was warm and slightly flushed. There was complete hypnosis. I took a chair, carried it over to the couch, and sat down on it with a smile of triumph.

"Are you listening to me?"

"Yes."

With her hair undone and her eyes wild, she exercised a curious sexual attraction. Could she feel pleasure?

As I had planned, I asked her what event in her life had produced the most lasting effect; her mother's death, she said. I asked her to describe this event to me in full detail, and this she did with every sign of deepest emotion—how, she began, they had all been together at a place on the Riviera of which they were very fond, and while they were crossing a bridge her mother had suddenly sunk to the ground and lain there lifeless for a few minutes, but had then got up again and seemed quite well; how the next day, or the day after, as Lucy was lying in bed, her mother, who had been sitting at breakfast at a table beside the bed, had got up all at once, looked at her so strangely, taken a few paces forward, clutched her stomach, and

fallen down dead. Every effort had been made to revive her—
Herr O had called in several doctors immediately—but it had
been in vain.

The patient then began speaking, without any transition,
of a large toad sitting squarely in the middle of the carpet.

"What are you speaking about, Lucy? There is no toad on
the carpet. Why do you see these hallucin— these animals that
aren't really there?"

"How do you know they're not really there?"

"Nobody else sees them."

"But what if they are really there and it's just that at the
moment neither you nor I can see them?"

"Nonsense!" Why was she asking me these questions? Was
the hypnosis wearing off?

"Why is it nonsense?" she insisted. "Isn't it possible that
the animals are really there, but that they're hiding in order to
trick me? You will at least admit the possibility?"

"No! Never! Only mad people think like that, not doctors.
The animals only want to annoy *you*, fräulein. They have nothing against me."

"Perhaps you are not looking for them hard enough."

"Deeper!" It was difficult not to scream at her. "You are
falling deeply asleep. Deeper sleep! Deeper sleep! You are
sleeping. You are deeply asleep. Tell me, Lucy, why do you find
these animals so frightening?"

"They remind me . . ."

"Yes?"

"It has to do with a memory of my earliest youth."

Apparently one day when she was five or six years old, she
and her father encountered a life-size stuffed bear on a side-

walk. The bear terrified her. To her father's fury, she refused to go anywhere near it. Afterward she saw some dead squirrels with their eyes hanging out and she remembered the bear. That was when she had her first fainting fits and lapses of consciousness.

"How old were you then, when all this happened?"

"I am a woman from another century."

"Please explain."

No reply.

"What do you mean?"

No reply.

"Lucy!"

"Yes?"

"Do you know what a phallus is?"

No reply.

"It is my belief that the toads and bears and other animals represent the phallus to you."

She began to sing: ". . . black man . . . holding me in his arms . . . up in a tree . . . father . . . nursed me as a baby . . . I remember his study with the sparking coil . . . Now the day is over." Something about the way she sang the song gave me a prick like a hot needle. I felt a thought rise up in me and swell into a lake, then fade before I could recognize it. I felt I was on the point of making a crucial discovery, a crucial confession to myself, but was holding back from such an irrevocable step as an admission of guilt. I felt like a murderer might feel.

I told the patient her personality interested me greatly. I told her I proposed to devote a large part of my time to her recovery. I said she was fortunate because the animal shapes she saw were only imaginary and temporary. I suggested that she should sleep well, that all her symptoms should get better, and so forth.

I stroked her several times over the eyelids, and her features took on a more peaceful appearance. She passed most of the afternoon lying quietly in bed.

This treatment by warm baths, massage twice a day, and hypnotic suggestion will be continued for the next few weeks.

---

23 August

A week of bears and fires and death's heads and pelting rain and damp black woods . . .

Today it rained intermittently right up to lunchtime. The whole region is veiled in a chilly mist, as on the worst days of October.

29 August

A confusion of feelings and fragmentary images—a strange yellow tree, an old cart-horse breathing fire like a medieval dragon . . .

8–10 September

Bad days, no impulse to write, constipated, too much to eat. Too tired to think of any wants.

I don't know what I want. Everything is quiet inside me and I feel terribly lonely; I must wait until something stirs and I can feel it.

I hate to be blocked, closed, shut. I want all the life of the

universe flowing through me. I want to let go, to lose myself,
my soul, what would it mean to feel life pulsing through me,
the big tides sweeping in till I'm one with the immense surging
fullness of the sea?

---

13 September

I was married to Martha Bernays, beloved granddaughter
of the chief rabbi of Hamburg, in the little town hall of
Wandsbek (see IV & V dream notebooks). We received 1,250
gulden from Aunt Lea in Brünn and 800 marks from Uncle
Louis Bernays in London, but all this has gone to cover the
cost of the furniture. The new apartment (four large sunny
rooms) is convenient for receiving patients, but so far I have
earned only 112 gulden in the month and need 250 for ex-
penses alone!

Thank God (and Breuer) for Lucy O; she is practically/
economically my only patient.

---

16 September

I want— Now, while wondering what I want, the patterns
and colorings on the vase on my table took on a new and
intense vitality . . .

I want to feel myself part of things, of the great drift and
swirl: not cut off, not missing things, not being sent to bed
early with the curtains drawn. I want companionship, another

soul to hit back the ball of my thoughts, but often when I'm
with people there's a fog and I can't . . .

I remember a feeling of always being cut off from other
people, separate, shut away from whatever might be real in
living. I always seemed to be looking for something, seemed
always a little distracted because there was something more
important to be attended to just ahead of the moment. But
what could life be? I want to feel I have "lived," I suppose—but
I don't want a life of service to a good cause, so it's no good
pretending I do. Maybe it's colossal egotism or my "condi-
tion," but I want a share in everything in the world, the bad as
well as the good.

---

20 September

Her period began and interfered with the massage. I put
her under hypnotic suggestion and set the interval at twenty-
eight days.

Under hypnosis, she seems to know everything that happened in the last hypnosis, whereas in waking life she knows
nothing of it.

---

23 September

I cannot understand why I am so terribly depressed, as if
there were no hope of salvation for me. Are the gods contend-
ing against one another deep within me? Is this pain a sacrifice
of the sort every great work requires? What work?

22–28 September

She alternated between periods of torpor and bouts of feverish energy during which she wandered about the grounds and drew or painted in enormous bound notebooks obtained from her father. Not once has she made any comment to me about her hypnosis, or asked me a single question about it.

―‖―

26 September

I was running down the path to the lake and everything was gleaming in bright sunlit colors. I stopped to catch my breath under the great old trees that bend down to the water . . . and suddenly I was reminded of home, the look and feel of the canal in the morning, the surprise of all the new ice glittering in the sun, and smoke rising like breath from the boats below. I was transported to a different realm, descending the wide smooth steps of a museum or temple and looking across at the shimmering city. There was a golden disk melting in the sky above me; the light was unbearably pleasurable, sunlight-as-moonlight. Through my astonished eyes the higher world flooded, untouched by fear or grief, or even happiness . . .

Then, suddenly, I was weeping in torrents, paying no attention whatever to the fact that several nurses and their patients were nearby. What did that matter to me? What was there left for me in this world? I must admit that it gave me great pleasure to weep in this way. I was longing for some comfort and everything came pouring out at once. Afterward

the air was cool and majestic. I breathed in the coolness ecstati-
cally. The trees, the grass, the people strolling by, everything
seemed grouped in an unusually picturesque fashion. I felt des-
tined for something great, felt above all petty concerns.

This feeling persisted until noon, when my first sustained
encounter with a live person dispelled the entire mood.

—◁—

2 October

In the evening she was cheerful and talkative and made fun
of her treatment by my medical predecessors. She asked me
many questions: about my wife, my friends, my medical theories, etc. It was almost as if she had adopted my inchoate
procedure of asking questions and was making use of our conversation, apparently unconstrained and guided by chance, as a
supplement to her hypnosis.

N.B. Last night (in a slight depression) I took coca again
and a small dose lifted me to the heights in a wonderful fashion. Truly it is a magical drug; I shall give some to Martha to
make her strong and give her cheeks a red color. (Important:
See if Merck can supply more at a low rate.)

6–17 October

Under hypnosis, heedless of my questions, she created stories and situations to which she would give me a clue with a
few muttered words or phrases. If I repeated one of these
phrases ("the girl has disappeared"), she would at once join in

and begin to paint a fuller picture, hesitantly at first and in paraphrase; but the longer she went on, the more fluent she became. Then, on the evening of the eighth, there appeared a deep-going functional disorganization of her speech, a kind of aphasia. For two days she was completely dumb. In spite of making great and continuous efforts to speak, she was unable to say a syllable. Binswanger gave me terrible looks and threatened to send for Breuer.

Then, during a session on the eleventh, under hypnosis, she was able to put words together laboriously out of four or five languages—a kind of exalted gibberish. When she tried to write, she employed this same gibberish. This state of affairs lasted through the fourteenth; gradually thereafter she began conjugating verbs and regained her command of grammar and syntax—but she spoke only in English, settling on this language without even knowing she was doing so. (It was only after many disputes that I was able to convince her she was speaking in English; fortunately, she had picked a language I could understand.) At first she continued to understand those about her, such as her nurses, who spoke in German; but this soon changed, so that even her father was obliged to talk to her in English. At rare times, when she was at her best and most free, she spoke French and Italian. (There was complete amnesia between these times and those during which she spoke English.) When asked to read French or Italian aloud, she produced, with extraordinary fluency, a bravura extempore English translation.

On the morning of the seventeenth, in English, under hypnosis, she told me she had been angry with me for interrupting her narrative in an earlier session. When I asked her please to be more specific, she said, in a definitely grumbling tone, that I was not to keep asking her where this and that came from, but to let her tell me what she had to say. I fell in with this, and she went on without preface:

Shortly before the Trojan War,
on the borderline of history and what came before,
the mists of the past began to reveal
human heroes as well as gods.

That voice! It was changed, deep, thrilling. The intonation was strangely formal, as if she were speaking from a great distance in a manner robust and elegant at the same time. There was a rhythm to the syllables that was completely different from everyday speech.

In Arcadia around this time
a daughter was born to the king.
Little guessing her fame would eclipse his own
and hoping for future sons,
the king ordered the child exposed
to die in the wilderness.
The queen, exhausted from the birth,
attempted fitful protest.
She was supported by her rustic court,
two spinster aunts, a toothless maid,
and an ancient midwife, who swore the baby,
though a girl, was tightly made as any man-to-be.
In the end, by the king's hand

the child was given to a palace guard,
taken to a forested hillside, and abandoned.

She had risen off the couch and was staring at me with a peculiar wild strained intensity. Her head was set back like a dog's. The flow of words had stopped. The pupils of her eyes pulsed with light as if enmeshed in the countless threads of a sudden dream. Power and tension flooded out of her into every part of the room. Her hands knotted and reknotted. She began a kind of deep grizzling growl in her throat—a sob, then the suck of saliva—exactly the sound of a sick animal whimpering. Then something burst in her and she stood gasping like a fish before me, thrown up by the tides of inner music onto a foreign shore. There was a tremendous silence, a silence impossible to repair again. We were both exhausted. It was a momentous experience. I felt somehow fecundated, as if I were moving again toward the light of self-recognition. I walked over to the writing-desk for an ampoule of morphine. I stood contemplating my future, the future of psychical analysis; then I knelt beside her and lifted the hem of her dressing gown. Slowly, I rubbed the flesh with alcohol. Slowly, holding up the syringe, I pricked the needle through the taut rubbery skin, drew back the plunger, and inserted the needle into her clean white thigh.

Later: I have sent to my old friend Fleischl for some texts on classical mythology (I hope my schoolboy Greek is up to the challenge). I have also taken a larger than usual dose of cocaine to settle my stomach and my thoughts, although it seems to be having the opposite effect. Who is this beautiful archaic hysterical girl? Some dispersed unselfcomprehending Sappho inflated with trancelike spirit? I feel altogether so passionate, everything in me is at present so intense, my thoughts are so sharp and clear, that it is impossible to keep calm. My head is spinning with colors and delirious magic. All my delight in the ancient world (buried for years) is bubbling into life again. I long for archaeologists, philologists. My intellect is soaring at its highest. Thoughts throng my mind that promise to lead to something definite—that seem to unify the psychological and the mythological, the normal and the sexual problems—then they vanish. I try not to hold on to them, since I know that neither their appearance nor their disappearance in consciousness is a real expression of their destiny. "The scales are dropping from my eyes." I am wandering alone through undiscovered provinces of mental life, traveling in a strange country, seeing wonderful things no one has seen before.

Three

5 Maria Theresienstrasse

26 October

"She has taken him from me. He's bored with me, he thinks only of her. We're never alone anymore, that girl's between us. All the time! All the time!"

"Martha dearest, I'm sure the Breuers don't—"

"Martha, do you want a fan? Or another glass of wine? It's so hot, we're all on edge, there's a storm in the air."

Breuer tapped on my wrist with his finger. "Actually, Sigi, I've been wanting to ask you about Fräulein O myself. This spoken dimension of hers, the oracular business you've alluded to—is it scientifically sound?"

"Why not, sir? Medicine has proved that human instinct is

unverbalized organized memory—not one's own memory, but the total of memories of countless anterior ancestral existences—and memory and voice are inextricably linked. If we could retrace our steps ten, fifty, a hundred generations, what would we find? The omnipotent authority of sound! For our ancestors, auditory powers were as uncompromising, as elemental, as wind, rain, fire."

"But the written word—literature . . ."

"Literature? The first people whom we call authors—the minds and voices behind Homer, the Bible, the Vedas—were public performers, for whom publication regularly took the form of recitation or incantation. The human voice reigned supreme until late in the second millennium B.C. Why shouldn't Lucy's auditory hallucinations be as real as her visual ones?"

"Well, as you know, Sigi, I've no objection in principle to regressive therapy by means of hypnotism. But until our physiological research has disclosed to us new properties of the nervous system, let us stick in the main to the well-tried methods of massage, baths, and electricity. Experience shows that no cure is possible outside of them."

"But, sir—"

"Let us be patient, and above all let us be modest—that is the first duty of doctors and men of science. Let us explore to the fullest hydrotherapy, electrotherapy, massage, the Weir Mitchell rest cure . . ."

"Oh, to hell with the Weir Mitchell rest cure! If there are unconscious mental processes—and you know there are—then some special instrument for investigating them is clearly required. The obvious instrument for the purpose is hypnotic suggestion."

"Perhaps—but mythology as well? You know, Sigi, in future months you may not find the mythical trail of crumbling footprints and cold droppings entirely to your liking. You're a doctor and you've no time to waste. *Cure* her—that is your first duty."

"Of course, sir, but I'm sure you agree that as a clue to psychological life, myths are potentially very useful. Lying on the borderline of what is known and what cannot be known, they deal directly in the stuff of consciousness—the stuff of memory itself. They prove that consciousness is only a hyphen—a tie between past and future, a presentation and accumulation of the past in the present. And like neurosis, consciousness seems to have preserved more mental antiquities than one would have imagined possible."

"Yes, yes, Sigi! But is Lucy getting better or worse? And what is she bearing witness to that refuses to be known by a more direct path? Do you believe there is actually some archaic relic in her?"

"I do believe it; and in some way I don't yet understand, it has become clear to me that we will not solve the ultimate secrets of neurosis without mythology. Perhaps what was seen in the prehistoric period gives rise to dreams and what was heard to myths . . . What do you think?"

But Breuer refused to be drawn into a theoretical discussion. Once or twice he asked for facts as if I were a recalcitrant schoolboy. Only the small amount of cocaine I had taken at the beginning of the evening kept me from baying at him like a wild dog!

If only they knew how much I myself am being moved forward almost entirely by unconscious forces and am very much at the mercy of them!

—✦—

28 October

Dr. F asked me if I like him! What could he have meant by that? I explained that of course I like him but I cannot help it if my proud nature resists his growing power over me.

(Father says a man like Dr. F can never sustain friendship in the long run. If I am nice to him, he will want love. This depresses me so much!!)

—✦—

2 November

I cornered Breuer next to an empty bed in the neurology ward and managed to reopen our conversation about hypnosis and mythology: "Perhaps not just with Lucy but in *every* case, behind the childhood of the individual, we are given a mytho-logical picture of the development of the human race in which the individual's development is only an abbreviated recapitula-tion influenced by the chance circumstances of life. Perhaps in individual fantasy the prime material and form are *always* mythic or mythologically typical. Perhaps prehistory itself is never any more than a group fantasy of the childhood of the individual. Perhaps pieces of the old religious pantheons are floating around in the inner lives of all of us."

Breuer considered this. "Then you actually believe these old stories are universal—a kind of universal complex? But aren't they inherently false, even by antiquity's standards?"

"Not at all. As scientists we have traveled in this matter far from ancient thinking and feeling. A 'mythos' to the Greek was primarily just a thing spoken, uttered by the mouth. It wasn't false, just oral and symbolic—visionary rather than enacted."

"Then it was . . . wasn't rational . . ."

"Mythology centers on the same nuclear complex as the neuroses and constitutes an essential part of their content. The nuclear complex of the neuroses is the nucleus of mythology, and vice versa; the *material* of myth is the same material that forms and animates the neuroses."

He looked at me with an equal blend of affection and condescension. " 'Animates'? That sounds more like biology than neurology, young man."

"Whatever you call it, whatever Aristotle would say, it is the primordial language natural to our psychic processes. Don't you see, sir? Our very instincts are mythical entities, magnificent in their indefiniteness, so that as physicians we can never for a moment disregard them or be sure that we are seeing them clearly. Myth-making is a reutterance and a preutterance, a regression to the subject's earliest condition, a revival of his or her childhood, of the instinctual impulses. But unlike the dream, which takes material from yesterday as well as from childhood, the myth life proceeds altogether from the relics of the prehistoric period, from birth to age three. It is the period that is the sole source of the unconscious, and the one that contains the seeds of neurosis."

"Sigi, you're a brilliant young man. It's just . . . sometimes you seem to lose sight of social reality."

"Social and political reality only recapitulates psychic mechanisms, sir. New and advanced powers only temporarily conquer indigenous ones, and always suffer an uprising of the primitive forces later on. To the ancients it was only through myth, through reference to the past, that life could approve itself as genuine and significant. Lucy O's song is the legitimization of her life; only through it and in it can her inner life find self-awareness, sanction, consecration."

⇥

5 November

  A bird glided down over my shoulder, the movement like a sudden music. I started laughing till the tears came just at being alive. (I'm writing this so when I'm sixty I'll not forget how I felt.)

7 November

  Wonderful visions partly of a terrifying cast but partly, too, of an indescribable grandeur. A deep voice saying, "Go to the sacred mountain where heaven and earth meet . . ."

⇥

At his invitation I dined with Herr O in an unusually large, well-kept mansion in Leopoldstrasse (a hotel? a brothel?). There was distant violin music as we entered the small dining lounge. The walls were hung with heavy wine-colored velvet and many oil paintings.

When we were seated I busied myself drawing patterns on the tablecloth with my fingernail and rubbing them out with my thumb. The waiter opened a bottle of wine and withdrew. Herr O came straight to the point. "My daughter has become moody and irritable. Do you propose to cure her by acting like a demented detective? Did you learn such things in medical school?"

"In Paris. From a man named Charcot."

"I have heard of him. He preys on poor unfortunate creatures who gain the attention of their doctors by absurd play-acting."

"Hysteria is not play-acting."

"No? Why not?"

"Because it always involves the connivance of the body."

"The body? Is that your specialty? The female body in particular? The neurotic wives and daughters of wealthy men and their supposed nervous collapses?"

"Perhaps this is a convenient time to ask about your wife's death."

"Another question from the past? You know, Dr. Freud, I quite believe you would do better to attend to your own secrets than to those that tend to exclude you by nature."

"What do you mean to say?"

"That it is evident to me you wish to tyrannize your patients, to become the monarch, the pope of the neuroses. That if I had to choose for myself, I'd a hundred, a thousand times prefer madness to enslavement. Are you so sure your own mind is sound, Freud? To probe the soul without becoming corrupted, one would need the purity of an angel. Take my advice and leave to the night that which belongs to the night—the darkness . . . But can a doctor's mind grasp all this?"

He was drunk, speaking in glacial tones as if none of this mattered or affected him in the least. Deep in his voice there was an inflection, a pause, a way of accentuating certain syllables, that reminded me of his daughter. I am a godless Jew, but I am sorely troubled by this case. The pen is heavy in my hand, the paper hurts when I touch it. I feel that I have drawn the curtains and am working by shaded light, like an acrobat in the semidarkness of a circus who performs dangerous new leaps in front of an imaginary audience before the public is let in. In some unfathomable way, Herr O and his daughter constellate the outlines of the problem. Why is he so defensive about her? Did he seduce her? In childhood? In infancy? Is it even possible? Again and again I am dragged toward the same conclusion. Again and again I arrive at the fertile field of infantile sexual trauma. But there is no proof!

Meanwhile my modus operandi, if I have one, consists of wiping away the worst of her animals by means of hypnotic suggestion. When she has described her hallucinations in detail, her mind appears somewhat relieved; but the scenes return the next day. Why? Is every attempt to formulate secrets and horrors, however incoherent, doomed to failure? What kind of work is this that revolves around the contents and forms of unconscious desires? Perhaps her father is right; perhaps I am only a male voyeur into the lush interiors of women. Perhaps I am practicing vivisection or something worse. Perhaps my method, when I finally find it, will be to make women fall in love with me in order to cure them.

Of this I am certain: psychology is a science of retrieval, a journey of return. Doctor and patient together, we must return victorious to the spirit, having descended into Hell. And from Hell we must bring back trophies. Understanding is one of our trophies.

12 November

THE AETIOLOGY
OF ARCHAIC REGRESSION/DRAFT A

Hypothesis: the Arcadians were the first individuals to emerge from group psychology—not gods on the downward road to humanity, but men and women on the upward road to divinity, exemplary beings in the chrysalis or incubatory stage of their divinity. As demigods, their steps toward full humanity (greater consciousness) gave rise to countless errors that led animals as well as men to perish sooner than necessary—but perhaps this always happens when something that is the property of the unconscious powers is torn out of its natural context.

Mythological tradition rarely sets forth any actual account of old events (that is the function of legend); instead, it acts in such a way as to reveal a wish-thought common to humanity, common and constantly rejuvenated. Myths correspond to the distorted residue of wish fantasies of whole cultures—the secularized dreams of young humanity. As I read this morning in Hesiod, the word "Oedipus" (Sophocles' famous king) originally meant "phallic demon," "swollen foot," "erected penis," or simply "erection." Very remarkable! Myths are the sexual theories of children!

It seems to me certain that the period of the Arcadian myths (roughly 2000–1500 B.C.) was ravaged by a constellation of primitive, uncivilized, instinctual, erotic impulses which formed the natural and indispensable intermediate stage between unconscious and conscious cognition. *This is the most crucial period of antiquity for psychiatry*—the period when anxiety and neurosis originated in the prohibition of incest.

Whatever the biological/social background of the incest prohibition (overpopulation?), the suffering of humanity during a period of repeated attempts at sexual domestication must have been immense—the pain must have induced the conscious subjugation of instinct—

Wait a minute—that can't be right—

No. No . . .

Sometimes I believe I possess fragments of a new way of thinking (and even feeling), but these glimpses of something new, at first so intense, so vouchsafed, have recently begun blurring with increasing details. Am I going too fast? How will I ever succeed in making fully comprehensible to others that which I myself see only with such difficulty?

Yet I feel I am making progress with her. I feel I am moving forward from the plots, characters, and settings of her present life and recent past—across the river of forgetfulness, the River Lethe—and penetrating the obscure, inchoate, shade-populated region of infant sorrows and instincts where she is still haplessly living.

15 November

The name! I have the name! This morning, under hypnosis, she began again at once.

> *The baby's cries abruptly ceased in sleep.*
> *At windy dawn a bear came searching for food.*
> *Stooping to nuzzle the shivering infant,*
> *she carried her off to the mouth of a cave.*
> *In the cave all was warm and close with love.*
> *The child Atalanta suckled at the bear's teat*
> *through the span of one fall and winter.*
> *Then, when spring came,*
> *using her hands and feet*
> *to twist and grip the bear's shaggy fur,*
> *she rode for hours by the river Ladon,*
> *laughing at the sunlight on the water.*
> *Now here it should be said*
> *the poorer people of Arcadia worshipped bears.*
> *Unschooled hunters, still wrestling with Greek,*
> *they preferred a totem to the Olympians.*
> *At winter solstice, a group of them*
> *forsook their friendly southern town*
> *to come to pray at Atalanta's forest home.*

A sudden series of convulsions and *tics douloureux* pulled her body from the couch to the floor. There was a prolonged silence as her attention gathered and relaxed, gathered and relaxed. I looked into her eyes and felt a glacial chill creep up my chest. Her stare was like the intense brilliant stare of a bird, reflecting in a mirror all the visible world but not for a moment returning my look, seeming to see me merely as one of a thousand small details that make up the whole picture.

But I had stopped really seeing her. I had the name— Atalanta. That was what mattered to me. (Should I eliminate everything pertaining to the patient's "real" biography and confine myself to the exotic inner world of the prehistoric child?)

Later: I have found a reference to "Atalanta, daughter of Iasius, the Arcadian," in Fleischl's Apollodorus.

Here is the text:

Apollodorus (1st Century A.D.)

When her father would have persuaded her to wed, Atalanta went away to a place that might serve as a racecourse, and, having planted a stake three cubits high in the middle of it, she caused her wooers to race before her from there and ran herself in the nude; and if the wooer was caught up, his due was death on the spot, and if he was not caught up, his due was marriage.

When many had already perished, Meleager came to run for love of her, bringing three golden apples from Aphrodite; being pursued he threw them down, and she, picking up the dropped fruit, was beaten in the race. So Meleager married her; and it is said that out hunting they entered into the precinct of Zeus, and there taking their fill of love were changed into lions.

N.B. There is a surprisingly large group of myths that tell of races to win the hand of a bride (usually a race among men, but here it is a race between the sexes). A repeated mythical pattern like this must correspond to some reality, some actual custom of racing to win the right to a woman. The obvious place to look is the Olympic Games . . .

Hurrah! According to both Pindar and Plutarch, the most ancient sporting festival of Greece was a pre-Olympic *women's* festival called the Heraea. Dating from an earlier system of time-reckoning by the moon, these female games consisted of a series of races among virgins to choose the "moon-bride" of an unspecified "sun-bridegroom." Now, at the later, historical Olympic Games, the sun-bridegroom was the victor in the chariot race. He would ritually marry his moon-bride under the name of Zeus and take a spin around the circus. (The chariot races at the Circus Maximus have also been positively associated with the courses of the heavenly bodies: the two-horse chariot race represented the course of the moon, the four-horse chariot race that of the sun, etc.) But something's wrong: didn't it seem strange that the sun and moon should drive together in the same chariot, since they never rise together in the same quarter of the sky?

As for Aphrodite's golden apples—

The golden ball is a recurrent image in Grimm and Andersen and generally symbolizes a supernatural cosmic radiance and sense of unity with the universe. Like the sun, the ball gives off energy from the inside: gold represents the supreme value, the creative force submerged in the unconscious.

Interesting that there were three golden apples (instead of two, for instance). The reference is sexual, of course; the number three has been confirmed from many sides as a symbol of the male genitalia.

That last phrase in Apollodorus, the one about the lions, remains a mystery; but I suppose it isn't important.

Four

Binswanger's
25 November
A changeable November afternoon, sunny but uncertain. At moments the sun shone in sharp outline against the curtains, highlighting the crossed threads, but then a gust of wind would fling a brief shower against the panes . . .

Later, in the night, I felt cold all over. Everything I thought was fearful and sinister, with a queer veil of horror between me and all I looked on, like the twilight of the sun's eclipse. I just waited to let it pass, keeping a close grip on myself, but immovable. There were queer ghoulish phantoms, and I could remember no pleasant things.

28 November

What should I hope for? My spirits are so dismally low. This afternoon one of the patients gave a concert (Mozart, Chopin), but while I tried to listen, clamoring demons surrounded me, deafening me, shouting, "This is not for you! You are a shrunken and imprisoned creature! Your emotions are only poor pale imitations! Never can this glorious flood of great feeling sweep through you and absorb you . . ."

29 November

It certainly is a great relief to write a diary. One gains at least a measure of self-confidence. I have not yet lost faith in my powers. I intend to cling to my belief that a great destiny awaits me. (Haven't I emerged from my tempests with all my golden dreams unscathed?)

After lunch. I was reading when I imagined someone staring up at my room with longing. I went to wash and closed the curtain in such a way that there was a gap through which he could look into the room. I didn't do it on purpose, but by the time I was at the washstand and noticed the mistake, I didn't feel like changing it. For the first time I took pleasure in having some of the contours of a grown woman . . . I was happy that my skin is soft, my curves just discernible. I felt myself blushing, and even as I noted this "objectively," it pleased me very much. What could be more beautiful than a healthy young girl, if she is maidenly?

I December

I've found two more references to Atalanta—not as a runner but as a woman who hunts. (Surely hunting was an unusual activity for a female? Not in Arcadia?)

Callimachus (Born c. 310 B.C.)

Further thou didst commend swift-footed Atalanta, the slayer of boars, daughter of Arcadian Iasius, and taught her hunting with dogs and good archery. They that were called to hunt the boar of Calydon find no fault with her; for the tokens of victory came into Arcadia, which still holds the tusks of the beast.

Pausanias (2nd Century A.D.)

Besides the exploits shared by the Tegeans with the Arcadians, which include the Trojan war, the Persian wars, and the battle at Dipaea with the Lacedaemonians, the Tegeans have, besides the deeds already mentioned, the following claims of their own to fame: Ancaeus, the son of Lycurgus, though wounded, stood up to the Calydonian boar, which Atalanta shot at, being the first to hit the beast. For this feat she received, as a prize for valor, the head and hide of the boar.

On the front gable of the modern temple of Athena Alea at Tegea in the Peloponnesus is the hunting of the Calydonian boar. The boar stands in the center. On one side are Atalanta, Meleager, Theseus, Telamon, Peleus, Pollux, Iolaus, the partner in most of the labors of Heracles, and also the sons of Thestius, the brothers of Althaea, Prothous and Cometes. On the other side of the boar is Epochus supporting Ancaeus, who is now wounded and has dropped his axe; by his side is Castor, with Amphiaraus, the son of Oicles, next to whom is Hippothous, the son of Cercyon, son of Agamedes, son of Symphalus. The last figure is Perithous.

The ancient image of Athena Alea, and with it the tusks of the Calydonian boar, were carried away by the Roman emperor Augustus after his defeat of Antonius and his allies, among whom were all the Arcadians except the Mantineans. The image of Athena Alea at Rome is as you enter the Forum made by Augustus. Here then it has been set up, made throughout of ivory, the work of Endoeus. Those in charge of the curiosities say that one of the boar's tusks has broken off; the remaining one is kept in the gardens of the emperor, in a sanctuary of Dionysus, and is about half a fathom long.

Of the votive offerings in the temple of Athena Alea at Tegea these are the most notable, but there is also the hide of the Calydonian boar, rotted by age and by now altogether without bristles.

N.B. Alea is a place name. Half a fathom is three feet or so —a sizable tusk! All the heroes on the front gable of the temple are of the generation *before* the one that went to Troy: Peleus was the father of Achilles, Castor and Pollux were Helen of Troy's elder brothers, etc.

4 December

Rain all day. I feel restless, at loose ends—a vague, tense feeling, such as one has when waiting for something with one's eyes shut. For the past few days I've been taking very small doses of cocaine against indigestion. It helps very much. (I actually believe cocaine can bring me fame and fortune. Do all its users feel this?)

A CONTRIBUTION
TO THE KNOWLEDGE OF THE EFFECT
OF COCAINE/DRAFT A

For at least four centuries, probably more, the leaves of the coca plant, *Erythroxylum coca*, similar to our blackthorn, have been chewed by South American Indian tribes in order to make themselves resistant to privation and fatigue.

The plant thrives best in the warm valleys on the eastern slopes of the Andes, six thousand feet above sea level, in a rainy climate free from extremes of temperature. In these conditions a healthy bush will yield four or five leaf crops annually and will continue to produce a yield for between thirty and forty years.

Coca arrived in Europe by a circuitous route. When the Spanish conquerors forced their way into Peru, they found the plant was cultivated and held in high esteem in that country. According to the historian Dowdeswell, the earliest recommendation for coca in Europe was contained in an essay by a Dr. Monardes of Seville, which appeared in English translation in 1596. Like the later reports of the Jesuit Father Antonio Julian and the doctor Pedro Crespo, Monardes' essay extols the marvelous effect of the coca plant in combating hunger and fatigue . . .

"How was Lucy today?" Martha asked me at lunch.

"Fine, thank you, Martha."

"Why not have a little try at hypnotizing me?"

"Don't be ridiculous! One doesn't hypnotize one's wife. It's a treatment, not a parlor game."

"Really? One doesn't hypnotize one's wife? What does one do with her, then?"

"You'll find out very well this evening what I have in mind for you."

"Is it true people can be cured by hypnotism? By commanding them to recover their health?"

"Perhaps. Why do you ask?"

"Will it bring you in more patients?"

"It will bring them in droves." I fondled my beard. "Let's see. Today is the sixth of December, 1886. How many patients does Dr. Freud have?"

"One, a sixteen-year-old girl named Lucy."

"A year from now, on the sixth of December, he'll have *fifty.*"

"Per day?"

I reflected. "That's a bit much. Let's say, per week. Do you take the bet?"

"What do I get if you lose?"

"If I lose, Martha, I'll give you a necklace with pretty golden balls on it."

"If you lose you won't have a penny to buy it with. Now finish your soup. And if you want to smoke between courses, go into your study."

9 December

After breakfast I went out and started running down the path that runs parallel to the riding trail. The grass was sodden with winter rains: I could feel the squelch of mud, see the ripples round my feet, the wet dead leaves blown by the wind, scudding like little ships in and out among the stagnant oozes.

I kept going, farther than I'd ever gone, following the brown curves. Suddenly I came upon an old house built sideways at the intersection of my path and a little stream. It was little more than a shed, really, with a look of being completely untenanted. I ran round to the back and there, in the little yard not two paces beyond me, a man was washing himself, utterly unaware of me. He was naked to the hips, his rough black breeches slipping down over his muscled slender loins, his slim white back curved over a bowl of soapy water in which he ducked his head.

I backed away round the corner and hurried back the way I had come. I was breathing hard and there were drops of sweat standing on my forehead. In spite of myself, I had had a shock. After all, merely a man washing himself—commonplace enough, Heaven knows! Yet in some curious way it had hit me in the middle of the body . . .

Was it the clumsy breeches slipping down over the white skin, the bones showing a little—or the way he was shaking his head with those quick strong motions, lifting his slender white arms and pressing the soapy water from his ears, quick, subtle as a weasel playing with water?

I suppose it was the sense of aloneness, of a creature per-

fectly alone, that overwhelmed me . . . the perfect solitary nudity of a creature that lives alone. And beyond that, a certain pure beauty of form, with curves and contours that one might actually touch: a body!

—

"How was she today?"

"Again! Martha! This is too much!"

"But naturally I'm interested! What am I supposed to do with my curiosity? I'm just asking if you've discovered any actual lesions."

"Martha, I've told you. She's a hysterical patient. She's under the sway of memories, ideas, and feelings that she's forgotten or of which she's never been aware. Her condition is one of emotive mimicry . . . fear . . ."

"She's putting on an act. Her real malady is lying. You don't believe she is malingering, just a little?"

"No, Martha. Not even just a little." I lifted her off the carpet, carried her into the bedroom, set her down again, and started covering her face with kisses. She yielded laughingly, but turned adroitly away when I sought to kiss her on the lips.

"Let me breathe. I've a feeling you're going to do something crazy with her. Don't . . . squander your future."

"I'm not crazy, Martha. But I feel out of the ordinary."

"Yes, yes. But you have no need to be a great man, because I love you."

"Kiss me!"

"I don't want to. You smell of cigars. Now leave me alone, you always spoil everything."

"Let me hold you close, Martha. You're so good for me! So good. There's no one but you who can cure me. You will cure me! I love you more than anything."

"You're cured. You're cured, Sigi. You're cured."

13 December

A CONTRIBUTION TO COCAINE, CONT.

Cocaine's wonderful, general therapeutic effects and uplifting qualities are ideal for physicians who have several drugs for calming excited persons but no safe psychic stimulant. The drug produces a lasting euphoria which in no way differs from the normal euphoria of the healthy person. The user is left with a feeling of buoyant serenity, an increased consciousness of being alive, an awareness of new bodily strength. He perceives an increase of self-control and he possesses more vitality and capacity for work. In other words, he is simply normal, and it is soon hard for him to believe he is under the influence of any substance. Absolutely no craving for further use of the drug appears after the first, or even repeated, taking of it; one feels rather a certain curious aversion.

13 December

Walking with my sketch pad I was drenched by a sudden shower of hail, and found shelter in the gazebo near the lake. I stood there shivering, pierced by the wind, looking out over the blackened landscape, thinking my own thoughts; suddenly I saw the man from the other day, half running, half walking toward me with a curious silent motion. He moved with a sort of aloof distinction, but also with a certain look of frailty.

As he saw me, he slowed a bit; then he continued forward with complete composure. I thought: Is he an underling? One of Herr Binswanger's hirelings?

"Good afternoon, fräulein."

"Good afternoon to you."

"You are a patient at Bellevue? I am Hans, one of the gardeners."

"My name is Lucy. How do you do?"

He said nothing.

"Do you hate being a gardener, Hans?" I asked him.

"Being a gardener, no! Why?"

"I should hate earning wages!"

"So long as I'm left alone. I don't like people!"

I watched him, his smooth dark hair and golden skin like the earth of Bavaria: he was like a swallow that has come to rest for an instant but is already trembling with the wish to resume its flight. The toss of his head, the way his arm moved . . .

Suddenly he rushed away from my side and out into the rain—the hail had turned to rain. Half turning toward me and glancing first at my face and then upward, he raised his hand to call my attention to something.

I craned my neck. Far up, as high as the tops of the tallest trees, a hawk was passing across the open space with loitering flight. In a few moments it was gone over the trees.

The wind continued to blow filmily but made little noise. The rain was abating. How green and alive everything was! All around the trees stood like powerful beings: dim, twilit, glistening, alive. It was as if the forest were stoically waiting for something, meanwhile giving off a potency of silence.

We set out from the gazebo and walked down to the water as the rain sank quietly into the lake and rustled softly on the leaves of the willows. I felt myself being floated away; it was as though the longing that filled me were a soft, light outflowing of my heart into an ocean of immeasurable peace. It was as though winter itself were dissolving; the water now seemed blue and light, rustling overhead on the leaves, hanging on the grasses in clear drops. A soft misty veil rose behind us, and when we turned round it had closed us in, so that in walking we seemed to be standing still. Slowly I leaned back against his chest as if he were a protective tree, bending back my neck. When he sank his head his lips touched my forehead; when he turned I felt his arms around me, his hands in mine, felt as if I were among the branches of a tree. His breath on my forehead was like the rustling of the rain. So motionless did we stand, so at one was the gray sky with the misty waters, that the foliage on the island in the lake seemed to float as in a gray insubstantial sea, hanging or resting there, I could not tell which.

Before he disappeared into the mist he raised his arm. Was this final gesture of his meant as a farewell? Was he forbidding me to accompany him? Or was there, perhaps, something more he would have liked to say?

She was standing talking to a man of perhaps twenty who was wearing black velveteens and brown shoes. It was around noon when I came upon them. She looked entirely normal and very beautiful. Perhaps her color was rather high, perhaps her expression was rather bedazzled and transfixed—perhaps it is only that she is one of those especially designed for sunlit ventures.

The man had his dark southern eyes fixed direct on hers and seemed to be sending out an appeal. He was lean and moderately tall, standing very still with that motionlessness of a race (Etruscan? Phocaean?) that can't be disillusioned any-more—an extreme, perhaps, of impurity that is pure.

". . . before sunrise. You promise, Hans?"

"If you wish it, fräulein."

That was all I managed to overhear. Was she speaking to him as to a servant? I could not be sure. Except for his curious far-seeing eyes he might almost be a gentleman, a separate sort of gentleman—alone, sure of himself, a free soldier rather than a businessman. As I approached, he lifted his hat, showing his thick, almost black hair; then, glancing into my eyes with a fearless impersonal look, he left.

I determined to say nothing about him; then, in the next moment, I decided the best approach would be one of psycho-logical frankness.

"Who was that, Lucy?"

"One of the gardeners."

"What were you talking about?"

"Nothing. One of the hunting bitches is about to whelp

and I was asking him not to drown the puppies." There was a pause. "You know, I'm not sure I want to be hypnotized anymore."

She turned and began walking toward the refectory. I bowed deeply and said goodbye to the air. Then I walked angrily down toward the lake and ran into that fool Binswanger.

"Who is your gardener? The young one with dark hair?"

"Hans? You've seen him here before."

"Yes, but where did he come from?"

"Nowhere! He's a Kreuzlingen lad. I was really very glad to get him. It's impossible to find a good man for a gardener, and it needs a man who knows the terrain."

"Nice weather we're having, eh, Binswanger?"

17 December

She expressed a feeling that in future she would be less obedient under hypnosis than before. To convince her of the contrary I wrote a few words on a piece of paper, handed it to her, and said, "At lunch today, which I am having with the patients, you will pour me out a glass of red wine. As I raise the glass to my lips, you will say, 'Oh, please pour me out a glass, too,' but when I reach for the bottle, you will say, 'No thank you, I don't think I will after all.' Do you understand? You will then put your hand in your pocket, draw out the piece of paper I have just given you, and find the words you have spoken written on it."

A few hours later the little episode took place exactly as I had prearranged it (and so naturally that none of the nurses or patients present noticed anything). When she asked me for the wine, she showed visible signs of an internal struggle, for she never drinks wine at lunch. When she had refused the wine with relief, she put her hand into her pocket and drew out the piece of paper on which appeared the last words she had spoken. She shook her head, and stared at me in astonishment.

19 December

I knew as soon as I saw her—even before I hypnotized her—there would be more poem. Why do I sense this infernal echo in her, this resonance in the soul which entwines me and her as if we were but a single note of music? Is she my creation, or is she creating me?

> *The leader of the hunters, Haralambos,*
> *had a fire built some distance from the cave*
> *and laid around it skins and skulls of bears.*
> *The little Atalanta spied the glowing*
> *in the hunters' camp.*
> *Stumbling forward on wobbly legs,*
> *she found the source of color.*
> *Pausing for a moment on the rim of pain,*
> *with light and heat already too intense,*
> *she jumped direct into the flames,*
> *emerging rapt, unharmed, unscathed,*
> *with penetrating hazel eyes,*
> *into Haralambos' arms.*

And so belatedly the human family claimed its own.
The customs of the time and place
gave girls as well as boys free rein
to plunge their bodies headlong into movement
and test themselves against the mountain world.
In time the growing Atalanta
learned to string a child's bow
and fit a tiny arrow to the string
and pull, and plunge the shaft
direct into a maple tree.
And for the training of her soul,
the worthy Haralambos found a woman, Herse,
of Calydon across the sea,
high valued for her play with memory.

At this point Lucy's voice cracked and a kind of duet
ensued (dual possession?). I'll try to indicate this with quota-
tion marks.

"Is the legend true about you?"
"What is legend?"
" 'Story-of-yourself.' "
"I don't know."
"Come. Compose yourself and speak."
"I don't want to."
"Tell me this at least:
are you Arcadian or Spartan?
You were not born of bears, I think.
To look at you, you are the favorite of one
immortally a woman and the child of Zeus.

Her name is Artemis, the swiftly riding moon,
the white-armed holy goddess of the ceaseless hunt.
You must accept and honor her, she is your special lord."

Listening to her, to the intense conviction that vibrated in her ringing passionate tones, I felt absolved temporarily from further objectivity. The girl was herself so near to the supernatural that she had brought it near me. Indefinable feelings, long latent in me, stirred into life as against my conscious will I followed the direction of her divine lustrous eyes. Peering at the sky through the window, I seemed to see in the distance another being like herself, a Lucy glorified, leaning her beautiful spiritual face to catch the winged words uttered by her child on earth.

Five

5 Maria Theresienstrasse

3 January 1887

Now this is really too much. I feel I am dissolving completely into pus! No less a writer than Euripides, the most psychologically acute of the ancient tragedians, wrote a play called *Meleager* or *Meleagros,* and Atalanta was the heroine!

Unfortunately, the text has been lost, except for the following fragments.

Euripides (480–406 B.C.)

1) "This is the fortunate land of Calydon with its pleasant plains, across the straits opposite the country of Pelops. Oeneus, son of Porthaon, rules over this Aetolian land; who wedded Althaea, daughter of Thestius and sister of Leda."

2) "Oeneus, obtaining an abundant harvest from the land, sacrificed the first fruits to all but Artemis . . ."

3) "It is fitting that a good woman should remain within the house; out of doors she is good for nothing."

4) "If men were to attend to the labor of the loom, and women were to take with pleasure to weapons . . . deprived of their knowledge, they would be worth nothing; nor we either."

5) ". . . swift-footed Atalanta, for whose sake Artemis let slay the boar, seeing she favored the maiden greatly."

6) "The goddess of love is a friend to darkness, for light makes needful chaste self-control."

7) "That which is strongest is virtue, even though that which is strongest be a woman; the name makes no difference."

8) "Arcadian Atalanta, hated of the Cyprian, had her dogs and her bow, and Ancaeus brandished a two-edged axe. Telamon bore a golden eagle upon his shield as defense against the wild beast, and crowned his head with clusters of grapes in honor of Salamis his fatherland, the country of goodly vines."

9) ". . . to do good to the living; each man or woman, dying, is earth and shadow; the earth sinks into nothingness."

10) "The world is flooded with light, but the world below is foul darkness."

N.B. Too bad there's not more on Artemis. "The goddess of love" in fragment 6 and "the Cyprian" in fragment 8 are Aphrodite—"Golden Aphrodite," as Euripides says elsewhere, "who stirs with love all creation / But cannot bend nor ensnare two hearts / Gray-eyed Athena who cares but for war and the arts of the craftsmen / Artemis, lover of woods and the wild chase over the mountain."

Apparently the essential Artemisian urge is the longing for freedom. Artemis never moves beyond the adolescent stage into full womanhood. When her father, Zeus, asks her what gift she most desires, she answers unhesitatingly, "Pray, give me eternal virginity." Her independence is her essential reality, not a transitional stage. She never allows herself to become the passive, hunted object of desire but continues the search for herself, for her spirit, in solitude and separateness. But she protects childbirth. She is mother to all that is young, wild, vulnerable—mother of everyone's youngest and fairest child, who is the soul, the spirit, struggling to be born.

12 January

As I knocked and opened the door to Lucy's room, immediately a scent of something (roses?) told me she was not alone. Standing next to the bed, gazing back at me with large gray eyes and gleaming brown lashes, was a lady of about my own age, perhaps a year or two older. Even my limited experience as a man of the world told me at once she was not just foreign but "sophisticated"—there was something glamorous and unique about her expression, the suppressed animation that played over her face and swam between her eyes. Though she deliberately shrouded the light in her eyes from her lips, in spite of itself it gleamed forth from time to time in a bewitching three-cornered smile. It was as though her nature were so brimming over with something that, against her will, it expressed itself now in a smile, now in a radiant look, now in a slight pout, now in a magnificent frown. I felt myself kindled by her like a taper.

Carrying her barely plump figure with extraordinary lightness, she advanced and introduced herself in charmingly accented English as Mrs. Sophia Schliemann. For some reason the energetic grip with which she boldly and vigorously shook my hand filled me with joy. She said something about her daughter Andromache (can that be right?) and a school in Switzerland called Le Rosy? Le Rosay?

Suddenly it dawned on me that this was the young Greek wife of the great Heinrich Schliemann, the discoverer of Troy! (Perhaps unconsciously I had recognized her wonderful dripping golden necklace from my well-thumbed copy of *Troy and Its Remains*.) I was quite overcome. He must be twice her age! I stammered out a formal greeting but only succeeded in interrupting the flow of her conversation. Apparently she has arrived from Berlin, where Herr Schliemann is recuperating from an ear operation.

Where is she staying? Why has she come? What is her relationship with Herr O? Has she been summoned?

＝＋

12 January

Tante Sophia has come to me with much fanfare. She is as vivacious as ever but for some reason I am confused about seeing her. Because of H?

At school when I dreamed in my loneliness of a girl friend, I always pictured her as being exotic, the best student in the class after me. Then such a girl actually turned up! Andromache! That summer, when I met Tante Sophia, I felt myself not only under her sway but in love with her, as young girls fall in love with married women. She was wonderful, not at all like a society lady, not even like the mother of a young daughter. Her spontaneity and her freshness made her seem more like a girl herself. She was completely natural! I felt that she was not trying to conceal anything, but that she had another and higher world of complex and poetic interests beyond my reach.

This morning I wanted to say to her, sometimes I feel so happy, so happy I would like to embrace the entire world, so happy I don't even appreciate my own happiness, instead throwing myself with so much energy into emotion that I grow weary and see everything facing me as dreary.

What is it I want? (There comes that difficult question again.) I suppose I want to see something, anything, clearly and hang on to it. I suppose I want time to draw and study a few things closely by feeling, not thinking. I want laughter, its satisfaction and balance and security; I want a chance to play, to do things I choose just for the joy of doing, for no purpose of advancement. I want to live among things that grow, not among machines. To understand patiently the laws of growing things. To live in a regular rhythm with sun and rain and wind and fresh air and the coming and going of the seasons. I want a few friends like H and Andromache that I may learn to know and understand and talk to without embarrassment or doubt.

The hardest thing is just to wish for something consistent. I suppose it's hopeless. I really can't reason anymore. But if not reason, isn't there something else—an intuitive sense of how to live, something like the instinct that prompts a dog to eat grass when he feels ill?

13 January

Sophia asked, "Do you love him a great deal?"

"My father? Well, yes, I do. With every fiber of my being. His displeasure is driving me mad . . . And yet, I wonder if I love him. Sometimes I think I hate him! Sometimes I say to myself, it's not possible to hate him so much. One of us two must be a monster; if it's not me, it's him."

Later: "C'est bien tout, ma petite?"

"Except for one thing, something I simply can't tell you without blushing all over."

"Really? Will you tell it to me tomorrow?"

"Perhaps, if we sit in the dark and you let me whisper."

"Are you keeping your diary, Lucy?"

"Yes, sort of."

"Keep going—and I think a diary should do more than record feelings, don't you? It should be a motive for experiment and observation as well."

Dear Merck,

Of *course* I share your hope of finding a useful centrally active drug without undesirable addicting properties, one that cannot be abused, etc. But I repeat: the present still artificially high price of your alkaloid is an obstacle to all further experiments.

16 January

I was informed after lunch that Schliemann's wife was waiting for me in the visitors' lounge. She was wearing pale green silk with darker green ruffles and a matching hat with pheasant feathers. As a figure swathed in almost imperceptible plumpness she corresponded precisely to my ideal of beauty, which is Hellenic, only with a bit more flesh on it so as to make the classical line a little less rigid.

"Dr. Freud." She smiled pleasantly.

"Good morning, Mrs. Schliemann."

"I hope you can understand my wish to comprehend Lucy's case. She is like a daughter to us, having stayed with us in Athens several times."

"Hysteria is a rather difficult and challenging business, I'm afraid, Mrs. Schliemann. Lucy suffers from scenes—hallucinations and nightmare-like states that invade her waking hours."

" 'Scenes'? As in an opera?"

"Not quite. You see, what once dominated waking life, while the mind was still young and incompetent, seems in our century to have been banished into the night. The primitive weapons—bows and arrows—that have been abandoned by adult men are turning up once more in the nursery. Fortunately, the state of sleep normally guarantees our adult security—except in a state of pathology, when the watchman is overpowered and unconscious excitations overwhelm us, obtain control of our speech and actions, and direct the course of an apparatus that was not designed for their use. This is the state in which Lucy has found herself."

"I am trying to understand you." Mrs. Schliemann's dark eyes fixed upon me with a steady ironic scrutiny. "It seems rather abstract."

I expanded. "Psychiatrists distinguish between two types of mental illness, the psychoses and the neuroses. Whereas the neuroses affect only feelings, as with neurasthenia or anxiety neurosis—or behavior, as with obsessional neurosis—the psychoses are characterized by deep disturbances affecting the personality of the patients and their sense of reality. Lucy's case is one of psychosis."

"I see. And how long does the treatment last?"

"It's difficult to say. There are cases of psychosis in which a complete or partial cure may be obtained without our having to go as deep as the infantile experiences—but Lucy's is not one of them."

"Infantile experiences?" Her very wide-set dark gray eyes were traveling over me, carefully avoiding my own eyes.

"My method with her, dear lady, is rather like putting together a child's picture-puzzle, or assembling a storybook of early experiences. Slowly the missing pieces are found, turned in the light, and fitted together."

"Yes? But you sound like an art collector, Dr. Freud! You sound as if she is a plaything for you, useful for your experiments, like some poor frog."

"Well . . . I am a doctor, madam, but psychiatry is not yet out of its infancy. Perhaps one day it will be possible to cure madness simply by acting directly upon the cells of the brain. In the meantime, since we are not at that stage yet, please allow me to point out some of the scientific assumptions on which our German medicine has made its not inconsiderable advances. First of all—"

"Then you subscribe completely to the Helmholtz canon of determinism and materialism?"

"Certainly. I have been trained in the tradition of Helmholtz, and it is this tradition that I am expected to embrace and ornament. To men of the Helmholtz school, the idea that the mind—not the brain, not the nervous system—might itself be the cause of its own malfunction, even the cause of the body's malfunction, is worse than a professional heresy: it is a profanation of thought."

"Tell me plainly, Dr. Freud—what is your hope for her?"

"That in time that which is genuine will gain the upper hand."

"No. I don't believe you. Your attitude is passionate, but too detached. You have warmth, but lack soul. It seems to me your German expertise puts her in an untenable situation."

"On the contrary, I do only what your husband has done repeatedly. Yes! Imagine that the great Herr Schliemann arrives in a little-known region where his interest is aroused by an expanse of ruins, with remains of walls, fragments of columns, and tablets with half-effaced and unreadable inscriptions. He would certainly not content himself with inspecting what lies exposed to view. He would dig! He would bring picks, shovels, and spades with him, and he would set the inhabitants to work with these implements. Beginning from the visible remains, as I understand his methods, he would build up the walls of the temple or palace from the foundations that are still standing, determine the number and position of the columns from depressions in the floor, and reconstruct the mural decorations and paintings from the remains found in the debris. Well, just so does the psychiatrist proceed. Just so does he draw his inferences from the patient's fragments of memories, as well as from her associations and her behavior; just so does he pose a rhetoric of psychological theory against the existence of archaeological fact. I believe something in Lucy suspends and abolishes profane time and institutes apocalyptic mythical time in its place. I believe her physical destiny somehow alludes to mankind's psychic one. Like all true hysterics, she is an inscription, a hidden message, which, when it has been deciphered and translated, may reveal an alphabet and a whole language of undreamed-of information about the events of the remote past."

"The past . . ." She spoke with a sudden wonderful animation. "Men and gods, we are of the same family; we owe the breath of life to the same mother. In the olden days meals were taken in common; men and the immortal gods sat down together; there was a commingling. Such things as private property and family did not exist. Earth herself gave us an abundance of fruits from trees and other green things, spontaneously and not through husbandry, and people dwelt naked in the open air, for the temperature of the seasons was mild. And they had no beds, but lay on soft couches of herb which grew abundantly out of the earth . . ."

Her words plucked at the most secret, sensitive chords of my body. I was acutely aware of her nearness. I imagined the heat of her breath on my mouth, my lips opening, her breath touching my tongue.

"I am not sure I like you," she said. "There is a certain bellicosity associated with your intellectual suppleness. You have the arrogance and ruthlessness of a man who is too conscious of his own vocation. By the way, would you mind if I found Lucy and her father a place to live for the duration of the treatment?"

She had caught me off-guard, but as I calculated that she was offering me freedom from that meddler Binswanger, I told her I would have no objection. (Rather like a shopkeeper, I suggested she "come again" to Lucy's sickroom at her earliest convenience. I am afraid I was absurdly enthusiastic in this invitation. I still squirm and emit low moans of remembered embarrassment.)

20 January

Hated to wake up. Felt extremely low. What's so awful about these states of depression is the lucidity, or at least apparent lucidity, that accompanies and reinforces them. Despair seems the only genuine response to the meaninglessness of life.

I've found another reference to the boar of Calydon, basically just a list of hero-hunters, but it shows again how odd a hunting woman was.

Anonymous (Roman Empire)

Now the men who had assembled to hunt the boar were these: Meleager, loved of Ares, from Calydon; Idas and Lynceus, sons of Aphareus, from Messene; Castor and Pollux, sons of Zeus and Leda, from Lacedaemon; Theseus, son of Aegeus, from Athens; Admetus, from Arcadia; Jason, son of Aeson, from Iolius; Iphicles, son of Amphytrion, from Thebes; Pirithous, son of Ixion, from Larissa; Peleus, son of Aeacus, from Phthia; Telamon, son of Aeacus, from Salamis; Eurytion, son of Actor, from Phthia; Atalanta, daughter of Iasius, from Arcadia; Amphiaraus, son of Oicles, from Argos.

With these came also the sons of Thestius.

N.B. "Meleager, loved of Ares" is interesting. Ares, god of war and strife, was Artemis' sworn enemy; she berated him as a "blockhead" and a "maniac." His birth myth is unexceptional: brought up abroad, tutored by Priapus, the young Ares returns to Hera, his mother, in order to sleep with her. Hera's attendants, not recognizing him, refuse him admission. He goes into the town, fetches help, overpowers the attendants, and sleeps with his mother. No surprise here. The lawless and resurgent male god (Ares, Adonis) is everywhere phallic (only Christ has been transformed out of recognition); but what does it mean for Atalanta? If Meleager represents the ravaging impulses of mindless hot-blooded aggression shooting out lustfully with no thought or restraint, does Atalanta incarnate a more conscious heroic striving?

What was the original family violence, the original sin?

("The sons of Thestius" were Meleager's maternal uncles.)

<hr/>

29 January

"Where would you go?" Hans asked when I mentioned leaving Binswanger's.

"I don't know, some house nearby. We'll be able to see each other." I ran ahead of him and crouched on my heels and watched the swifts circling high up against the pale sky, their wings gold-bronze catching the early sun. I wasn't particularly interested; I recognized them as "just birds" and watched first one and then another. Then, with H behind me and the sun still rising, something opened in me. Everything, my whole attention, was gripped by the pattern and rhythm of the swifts' miraculous flight, their slow sailing, which had become a wide majestic dance. I felt all life flowing around me, through me, over my head, under my feet. It was one of those "moments," as one calls what one cannot describe. I wanted it never to end; I would have been happy to stay in that place forever.

"Are you happy?" He pulled me to my feet. I nodded yes but kept my head down (his asking made me feel shy). He laughed and made me a sort of bow but said nothing at all. For several moments he remained still, and I thought I detected in his dark impersonal eyes a look of detachment. Why is he so aloof, apart?

He shifted his weight and suddenly his face was close, his eyes worried. He's rather frail, really. Curiously full of vitality, but a little frail and quenched.

He exhaled loudly. Then he picked me up in his arms and walked with me a hundred yards or so, carrying me easily. I marveled at his strength, because I am almost as tall as he. When he put me down, I could not catch my breath to speak. We continued on, and a vague sweet thrilling sensation of happiness and expectancy which had been carrying me higher and higher all this time now caught fire, until my mind was like a bright toy balloon that had broken loose and was floating, gloriously radiant, high up toward the sun.

⚊⧾

5 February

Even before seeing her I knew there would be more poem. Why? Do I suffer from 1) hysteria, 2) obsessional idea, 3) hallucinatory confusion, 4) paranoia?

Hypnosis:

From this time forward in her secret life
a picture of the goddess,
chaste and lovely, flashing through the woods,
began to move in Atalanta's heart,
as swift and clear and radiant as the moon
among the stars.
It drove her to explore the hunt
in earnest and in swift pursuit
of skunk and antelope and deer

and her own *Lady of the Wild Things.*
Puberty approached; the men of Tegea,
awestruck at her raven hair and alabaster skin,
perceived her special shine and went their separate way.
Then one day when she was tracking game alone
while other girls her age sat spinning thread,
the maiden fell asleep as if by spell—

She rose off the couch into a standing position. Cold spiders
of panic crawled down my back.

Two satyrs,
smallish well-formed men with tails
and thickly muscled goaty legs
and pointed ears and cloven feet,
observed the huntress on the forest floor.
Congratulating loudly each the other,
pleasure-bound to ravish her for sport,
they clucked their tongues repeatedly
and rubbed themselves against the olive trees.
But Atalanta wakened just in time
to seize her bow and climb
to that one spot, a rock as tall as she,
that gave advantage to the sudden scene.
Afraid to stand her ground for long,
afraid to flee in face of superhuman speed,
she fit first one and then a second arrow to her string
and shot them to the very centers of the satyrs' hearts.
And then the sky began to blacken and the moon appeared,

and hardly knowing what she did or why,
the maiden dragged the lifeless bodies to her rock
and prayed: O Goddess, Artemis,
protector of the young and pure,
if you have heard me from afar
come nearer now.
You see what I have done,
that they lie bleeding
and are swiftly dead.
It is a dreadful thing
and yet I beg you, please
break not my spirit with remorse
but take their lives as sacrifice to you.
Become my heaven friend and ally.
Let me imitate your days and weeks,
this clean, this strong, this true
to the unblamed end.

Six

Binswanger's
5 March
Sophia's found us a house! (What if it brings me happiness?)

Cranes
14 March
Moving day! And it's spring! The waters have subsided, the paths have become dry, the sunshine has grown strong, its warmth has penetrated the earth.

Met H as planned and ran east along the river path away from the house. After a while it was as if we had been wafted away into a morning of midsummer. The weeds gleamed emerald green in the warm sunshine, small birds twittered in the trees. An incredible silence descended on us. There was an air of enchanted passivity to everything. Not a breath of wind stirred, not a leaf-bud quivered, not a grass blade swayed. I seemed to be on the path of adventure, the path I had read about in books, the old lane choked with undergrowth. Old memories stirred inside me, old dreams, old words, dim relics of sensation, ancient lands, a confluence of pastoral images from the forgotten history of the world—ancient castles, shady avenues, autumnal gardens, vast horizons blending in a golden mist.

We stopped to rest at the foot of a hill and gazed around at the panorama of open fields and willow groves. Farther away were the water meadows, lace-edged in the wonderful radiant light, and beyond them the estuary winding toward Vienna, a blue distance streaked with gold. The house itself was in a hollow; around it were deep meadows and embankments full of birds and willows like egret feathers tucked about like piles of green cushions. I could just make out the dairy, the barn, the chapel, the boat house, even the dog kennel—all very vivid and neat, all shimmering in the dazzling glare.

"Why is it called Cranes?" I asked.

"No one really knows. It's just the local name for the house. It must have gotten into the deeds at some point. As far back as anyone knows it's been owned by a woman, and there's always been legal trouble over it."

"Are there cranes still?"

"There are one or two left; I saw a pair of them last year."

"It's so extraordinary that we should ever have met!"

"Lucy! Really?"

"Because I'm not afraid of you! Why are you so gentle?"

"It's become a principle with me to yield to my fear of

people. I am silent, or I avoid them . . . or I propitiate them."

"Are you propitiating me?"

"Oh, with you, I've long ago decided to yield to my cowardice." The noon had become afternoon. Never was there a more beautiful day!

(Afterward I felt the slight depression that follows a day that has been almost too perfect.)

———

21 March

A curious hour in which Mrs. Schliemann paid a courtesy call on Martha (to spy on me at home?). Seated before the unlit candles in the half-light of the dining room, the Greek woman was a power, a presence, a strange white figure among the living furniture. My bride seemed to flow back, almost like liquid, from her approach, to sink helplessly away from her. There was a noticeable silence between the two and a strange tension of hostility; they always kept a gap, a distance between them, as if they wanted always to be free each of the other— yet there was a curious heart-straining toward each other.

No message from the Os; they're still "settling in."

1 April

The note from Herr O was unnecessarily peremptory, so I kept the coachman waiting half an hour before entering his barouche.

Our destination was a kind of outlying suburb of villas, an imitation of the English model that is spreading rapidly in Vienna, though only rich families accustomed to a permanent equipage can live there without being keenly aware of the disadvantage of its distance from the city.

After three or four miles of skirting fine villas and gardens, we turned through an open gate into a park of more than a thousand acres of natural woods, protected by a high wall (except where the river formed the boundary). There were clumps of oak and ilex, with Scots fir growing among the deciduous trees, then farther along the woods gave way to orchards and lawns and ornamental lakes. There were successive waves of ribbon grass and periwinkle, then thousands of tall, narrow blossoms, white fading to cream fading to gold.

The house itself was in the half-timbered *style anglais.* Looking at it, I experienced a crystalline moment, realizing that I suffer not just from the creative nature of my therapy, but from the marginality of my social position. Rather than my having the power of life and death over the patient (symbolically the infant), it is all reversed. *I* am financially dependent on the patient; *I* am the governess. Naturally I am unwilling to accept this role: I want "in," I want to move into the patient's family, to become a kind of phallic mother. I don't know my place, which is outside. I don't feel the proper subservience—of a man who does, after all, belong to the intellectual elite— toward the possessors of horses, lands, traditions. Unfortunately, I *do* feel my ever-readiness to slave for these possessors, to lavish the charm of my individuality, the stores of my experiments, and my knowledge upon them, to adorn their houses, to edit their ideas, to serve them as clerk-of-the-works, secretary, coach, reader, eyes, hands, buffer, handyman—all without a thought of protecting my own interests by demanding preliminary agreements in writing, such as the right to publish Lucy's cure.

I was admitted by the butler, who whispered "the magician" under his breath to one of the footmen. I felt more like a disreputable medicine man than like a real doctor and wondered if in future I would be admitted by the front door. I waited five or six minutes; then I was taken to a landing where there was an enormous mullioned window overlooking a flower garden. I glanced out at the blazing mass of color. The effect was blinding: arches and trellises and terraces of spring crocuses and daffodils and hyacinths and forsythia, massed one on top of the other in ordered glory. It was a display that would have done credit to a bulb-grower's catalogue. Beyond was the wide swift river, shallow as a ford, almost obscured by the show.

A tall blond footman led me up stairs and along corridors. Although I was quite well dressed, I felt myself being sized up by every look and glance that I encountered (it evidently did not occur to anybody here to mistake aristocracy of the mind for the real thing). In Lucy's white-paneled bedroom I scrutinized the simplicity of the decor with curiosity. It was the room of a stylish, sensitive young woman. There were mirrors, easels, dressing tables, a bed, a bed-settee, wing chairs, high shelves of books running round the walls—and three large windows, all wide open, letting in the sunny air.

"Good morning," she said in her most self-possessed manner. She was dressed in a light-colored gown.

"Good morning to you, Lucy."

Setting down my bag, I moved to establish my authority with her in this new setting. I led her to the bed-settee and, with a light pressure of my fingers, wordlessly compelled her to sit down, then stretch out on it.

"Clasp your hands together, Lucy. Fingers laced."

"Very well."

"You cannot separate your hands."

"I can!"

"No! You can't any longer, because you're asleep. Sleep deeply. Deeper. Deeper!"

Hypnosis:

Early the following morning Haralambos
bartered water for a pair of hunting dogs
and offered them to Atalanta on a twisted leash.
And place was found for her among the hunting men.
And with the men she ranged far,
from wooded Mount Lycaeus
to the Spartan border.
In a year she was the best of them,
for none could match her perfect aim
and swift impeccable pursuit.
Then in the month of intermittent rain,
as Atalanta and the hunters camped beside a mountain pass,
a delegation arrived in Tegea from Oeneus of Calydon,
the richest and most celebrated king in Greece.
Dismounting at the house of Haralambos,
for it was he who spoke for Tegea, as everyone knew,
Clymenos spoke his business in a worried tone—

There was a pause, then she interpolated a series of moans and shouts (overlays?). Then she stopped all utterance and assumed an upright, contrite posture on the bed-settee, her arms tucked tightly between her knees. "May I be brought out of clouds?"

Something was terribly wrong. She was asking to be wakened from her hypnosis (the first notice she has taken of it while being hypnotized). Full of foreboding, I gave her one or two positive suggestions and passed my hand across her forehead.

"Wake up! Open your eyes, Lucy."

I bid her farewell, stepped into the corridor and ran into Herr O. (Had he been listening at the door?) He greeted me graciously and led me to a kind of widow's walk on the roof.

"I bought this telescope to investigate reports of a new species of large bird that has been spotted down the estuary."

To please him I put my eye to the telescope. Tree by tree, reed-patch by reed-patch, I turned my gaze upon the land. The water meadows lay mysterious and silent in the afternoon light. As I watched, their long vitreous expanse was filling up with winged visitants like some great terminus.

"They're called the birds of Aries, because they migrate after the vernal equinox."

"Fascinating."

"They come up over the Black Sea to the mouth of the Danube every year about this time—larks, ducks, kestrels, harriers, grebes, swifts, coming up in their millions across Asia Minor. At night—I don't sleep well—I hear them landing— the slither of wings on the river, the soft whewing of large creatures flying overhead in the clouds, the thick whirring of mallard wings, the metallic *kraonk kraonk* of high-flying geese. And it's not just the migrants. In the reception rooms you hear the constant chuckling and nattering of rooks and wood pigeons and owls and pheasants and partridges and whatnot. My God! What a constant background murmur they keep up! And the house is full of insects and bees coming in to lay their eggs or die or both; you see them on sunny days in front of the windows on the south and west sides, bees and dozens of wasps and hundreds and hundreds of tiny fruit flies. I detest things that fly. The servants have standing orders to open and shut the windows and flap at them with dusters. Of course, I don't like people, society—but if they will come, at least they will get some decent shooting! Yes! If I can do nothing else in this rented house, I will play the part of head gamekeeper."

Later: I have turned on the light to take down a dream.

While alone on a journey I was suddenly seized by an overpowering vision of a leaf-bearing tree, but without fruit. But the leaves themselves had been transformed by the effects of something (frost?) into sweet grapes full of healing juices. I plucked the grapes and gave them to a large waiting crowd . . .

The whole thing had the shimmer of destiny, as if it were a warning from the gods. What was in the grapes, cocaine? Golden grapes? To make a fortune, does a man have to live on his nerves in a perpetual state of intellectual fever, in a landscape where the only comfort consists of the sight of gold just out of reach?

Seven

"Come see what I've done to the dairy."

"On one condition, Sophia—may I call you that?"

She looked at me with those great gray eyes of hers. "What is the condition?"

"That we not talk about Lucy."

She laughed and led me along a charming brick path to the disused dairy. The door was locked, but she produced a key and we went in through an opening that could easily have accommodated a hay wagon. I gaped shamelessly: the whole thing was of solid oak and the same size and shape as the barn nearer the house. It had proved too big for a guesthouse or studio, and after various experiments the previous owner had constructed in the northern transept a studio within a studio. The place where we were standing was some eight feet above the rest, with a huge floor-to-ceiling window at our backs. A carved balcony, railed and balustered, prevented one from falling from the smaller room into the larger, and turned at one end into a graceful staircase. There was little design and no pretense, but great comfort and an airiness unusual in such apartments.

"Would you like some wine, Sigmund?" She poured something red from a three-footed gold flacon apparently representing a woman, for it had breasts and a navel.

"Is that flacon from Troy?"

"Yes, it came out of the ground filled with buttons and bracelets and finger rings, all of the purest gold. I'm still cataloguing them."

She spoke modestly, but everyone knew Heinrich Schliemann had found more treasure than anyone deserves to find. He had begun his career in a grocer's shop in Fürstenberg, retailing butter, milk, salt, coffee, sugar—famously sleeping under the counter at night to end up a millionaire merchant. Just as some people seem to have the power of divining water, he had a sixth sense that told him where gold was buried. Luck helped him, luck and a fierce hunger for gold.

The luck held in his choice of a second wife.

Wishing to marry a young Greek girl, he wrote to a bishop of the Greek Orthodox Church in Athens; again he struck gold. In all the world there could hardly have been a woman as sympathetic to and understanding of his needs as the wife selected for him. He has the Midas touch.

"I read somewhere, Sophia, that the problem that chiefly

occupies your husband's attention is the sale of his Trojan treasure."

"Nonsense, the treasure is beyond price. What price can one pay for the Sistine Chapel? Anyway, it all belongs to the Great Mother, Artemis-and-Aphrodite-in-one."

"Artemis-and-Aphrodite-in-one? I can't quite place the term."

"It was one of the Mother's names in pre-Hellenic times, before the Trojan War." She went to a carved chest and took out an elaborate gold diadem. Across the front were multiple rows of pendants adorned with leaves; on the sides were chains designed to cover the temples. She placed it on her head. It fit perfectly. Helen of Troy was never more beautiful.

I stammered, "I . . . I remember the burning debate in the newspapers on the 'Homeric question' . . . when your husband forced the world to accept the historicity of the siege of Troy."

"The mistake most people make is not to take the myths literally enough. What has been truly believed in becomes a fact of history, not a myth."

"Does Homer say anything about a Calydonian boar hunt?"

"Yes, it's in the *Iliad.* Would you like me to read it to you?"

It was difficult not to bleat or squeal. I felt that almost terrified excitement and delight that always heralds the advent of new truth.

Homer (? 9th century B.C.)

For upon their folk had Artemis-of-the-throne sent a plague in wrath that Oeneus offered not to her the first fruits of the harvest in his rich orchard land, whereas the other gods feasted on hecatombs; and it was to the daughter of great Zeus alone that he offered not, whether haply he forgat, or marked it not; and he was greatly blinded in heart. Thereat the Archer-goddess, the child of Zeus, waxed wroth and sent against him a fierce wild boar, white of tusk, that wrought much evil, wasting the orchard land of Oeneus; many a tall tree did he uproot and cast upon the ground, aye, root and apple blossom therewith. But the boar did Meleager, son of Oeneus, slay, when he had gathered out of many cities huntsmen and hounds; for not of few men could the boar have been slain, so huge was he; and many a man set he upon the grievous pyre. But about his body the goddess brought to pass much clamor and shouting concerning his head and shaggy hide.

"Is that everything?" I asked.

"I agree that one would like to know more."

"You mean there's nothing about Meleager falling in love with Atalanta? Wasn't it *she* who killed the boar? I'm sure I read somewhere she was 'the slayer of boars.' "

"You're forgetting, Sigmund, that Homer was a revisionist. He derived his authority not from the maternal moon, which had inspired all previous poets, but from the patriarchal sun."

"And so?"

"And so he ignored or truncated many of the old matrilinear myths to justify recent social changes—including the Atalanta myth. Atalanta belongs to an older generation, a generation steeped in the Minoan-Mycenaean world."

"Wasn't that around 1500 B.C.?"

She nodded in an infuriatingly sagacious manner.

"Yes. It was a time when women and men were still innocent, where a pure fire burned in their veins—before they became intimidated by guilt and terror and the endless repetition of tragedy. Divinity seemed within their grasp, a thing as light as air, as palpable as flesh, resembling perhaps the glimmering flames of campfires at night, the gleam of bronze, the shining of the olive trees. Each stream possessed its attendant nymph, every thunderclap was a word from a hidden god. Rivers, seafoam, mountains, trees—all living things partook of divinity."

"What about death?"

"Death was an error marked upon the face of the world; from death the Mycenaeans recoiled with bated breath and shuddering horror. But hating and fearing death, they were still capable of regarding it with laughter and flashing eyes."

"How do you know so much about them?"

"Because, I suppose, in casting his veil over the Mycenaean age, Homer more or less reveals it to us. He holds the mirror up to nature. The world he describes is the world of today."

"Meaning?"

"Little has changed in the thirty centuries since the burning of Troy. The fires burn, the besieged make their desperate sorties; everywhere the cries of the doomed can be heard. We are all Trojans. Homer, the blind wanderer among islands, describes our present plight with excessive brightness."

"But he was a writer . . . literature . . ."

"His voice made history; it was powerful enough to carry the shapes and colors of an entire civilization with it."

"But . . . but . . ."

"The life Homer portrayed was so rich, so stark, so majestic, so filled with sensuality, that men came to believe it wore the aspect of a dream. Then Heinrich Schliemann came along and staggered everyone by showing that it was a waking dream. It had all happened in the sunlight of the Ionian seas. The gold was real."

Really she is impossible. She makes no sense at all. She has a divine reverence for her husband and believes he has made the greatest discovery of the age. "He works by instinct and enthusiasm, like a woman, feeling his way into the past."

Yes, I wanted to scream at her, and his weapons are guile, cunning, patience, loquaciousness, and *money.*

6 April

Schliemann's impossible wife is right about Homer's suppression of matriarchal culture; the evidence is everywhere. "I honor the male in all things," he has Athena say:

> "This too I tell you, mark how plain my speech,
>   The mother is no parent of her child,
>   Only the nurse of the young seed within her.
>   The male is parent, she as outside friend
>   Cherishes the plant, if fate allows its bloom."

What a literal refutation of *Mutterrecht* culture! (Athena-Ares-Artemis-Aphrodite! All these A's! I can't get to B!) Homer's family of Olympian gods represents the form of society we ourselves are most familiar with. Zeus is head and phallus. Despite constant unseemly conflict (his wife, Hera, is indigenous and represents a matrilinear system; she is a turbulent native princess coerced, but never really subdued, by an alien conqueror), there is no doubt about his ultimate supremacy.

It is evident that Olympus was, to begin with, a home for mountain men in northern Thessaly. (As both father and sky-god, Zeus projects a specific northern racial influence.) Before Troy, in most of mainland Greece, there were only group marriages of all female members of a particular totem society with all male members of another; every child's maternity was certain, but its paternity debatable and irrelevant. Gradually, as the classical period approached, men took over many of the sacred practices from which their sex had debarred them and declared themselves head of the household, though much property still passed from mother to daughter. This was the transitional stage between matriarchy and patriarchy—the period of Hellenization, the period of repression of the mother principle.

Artemis easily outlived Athena and Aphrodite. She survived until the first century A.D., when Paul of Tarsus suppressed her worship and established a cult of Mary in a basilica at Ephesus adjacent to the ancient Artemision. This was the third stage of cultural development—the purely patriarchal, in which there are no goddesses at all; the stage of later Judaism, Christianity, and Mohammedanism.

Sophia: "A man cannot give birth. He cannot know the

end of his seed, whether it grows into life or not, unless he owns the woman he endows. As a result we have come to be governed in practice by the unholy triumvirate of Apollo, god of science; Hades, god of wealth; and Hermes, god of thieves."

8 April

Hurrah! No more Merck! I have received 100 grams of cocaine *gratis* from Parke Davis & Co. in America! Hurrah for the greater availability of coca leaves in the New World! And the product is not only equal to but even seems preferable to Merck's—more soluble, aromatic, pure white, free of hygrine, etc. It produces the characteristic coca euphoria—even more so!

11 April

A dream:

I was in a far place bathing in a pool of red water. I heard, "Now you must wait. Be still. She may enter you in any way. Something will happen. It will be your knowledge of the Mother."

Then I was clinging to an oak tree. The branches quivered with life. The leaves were like tongues, whispering some language I could almost understand. I ran my fingers over the bark. Every part of the forest seemed to fall asleep. Time seemed to whirl and yet to stop, as if I were at the center of everything.

At dawn I was awakened by steps on the grass. There was a

wild cow before me. I could see clearly her swollen udder, the thick yellow milk squirting from her teats. She gave no sign that she had noticed me. She started to hunch her back and paw the earth. Each time she hunched she gave a loud cry and panted like a huge dog. The panting came in short underbreaths.

Suddenly the cow collapsed onto the grass. I heard a deep rumble from inside her, a low humming noise coming from her throat. Dry froth crusted around her lips, and from her womb a dark fluid ran. I could see a movement, a growing wider and wider, as if something were coming toward me.

Still the calf did not come. The cow's breathing was so rough that I thought she would die. I looked directly into the birth hole: the opening was wide enough that I could see within it some movement. Instinctively I reached in; I turned something; the baby's head appeared, covered with slime, sliding toward me, steaming, blood-fragrant. I felt a mysterious lifting of my heart. I took some deep breaths. Heaving up on her legs, the cow stood trembling, with a bloody stream of flesh hanging from her womb. Nudging her calf to its feet, she raised her head and looked calmly into my eyes. I felt I had helped the earth to move. I felt the mysterious air breathing all around me like a pure misty vapor, like a glass of cold water, which I now drink.

—⊢

13 April

The day was windless and bright, with only a few white clouds floating at a great height above. Lucy greeted me with a dazzling Sophiaesque three-cornered smile and led me to a spot away from the house where a plush damask sofa from one of the drawing rooms had been placed on the ground like something exotic reared in a hothouse.

When I endeavored to hypnotize her, she at first resisted. Indeed, it was only after I murmured the word "Calydon" that she began declaiming with enthusiasm, even switching to the present tense (she had broken off with the appearance of Clymenos; apparently his business in Tegea had been to recruit Atalanta for the boar hunt).

Hypnosis:

In Calydon, despite the streaming glory of the spring,
the land remains unsown to thwart the raging boar.
The people bow their heads and openly despair,
safe at home but living even there
under the sway of passion-governed Artemis.
Before the tall and fluted columns of the palace,
drawn by love of glory, lust for fame,
and their undying mortal wish to imitate the gods,
the crown of men, the noblest youth of Greece,
stand sleekly at their ease like spoiling dogs
before a noontime fight.
Meleager is the first of them,
a driven, burning man of seventeen,
beloved of blood-stained war-god Ares,
son and heir of Oeneus and Queen Althaea.
Beside him, jealous of his early fame,
Meleager's uncles, Althaea's younger brothers
Toxeus and Plexippus, survey the scene.

In front of them, Ancaeus, Spartan hero of renown,
and Telamon of Salamis converse, a golden eagle raised
upon the latter's outsized shield.
Eurytion, a king in east Aetolia, is here;
Androgeus and Theseus and Jason;
Nestor, prince of southern Pylos,
oldest of the chieftains who will go to Troy;
Laertes, island-born at Ithaca, the sire of Odysseus;
bold Peleus, great-souled and with a mighty will,
the future father of Achilles;
Pirithous, king of the Lapithae;
Castor and his brother Pollux, twins of Leda,
loved of Zeus, on steeds of purest white—

The names! She was demonic! She grew more, more . . .

And now she comes,
last chosen and the last to take her place,
swiftly over the dark and unfamiliar sea;
northward across the swollen river Euenus,
and by a foaming moonlit sea-change
never more a child but a woman grown,
with glittering arms and glittering legs
and fire-swift eyes and fastening lips
and ivory arrows rattling in an ivory case
and twain hounds pulling on a twisted leash,
Arcadian Atalanta of the hills.
The hunters stare in wonder at her beauty.
One of them, Meleager, neither stirs nor draws a breath.

And slowly all around become aware
Meleager drinks desire as the woman moves.

There followed three voices: the first male, the second and third female.

"O Mother, she has finally come,
one feminine of sex yet faultless like a god.
Of women I have known and have not loved,
she is the most unlike and like to me."

"Meleager, love this swift and steep
will topple youth and lead to doom.
A woman armed for hunting
seeks not love from you or any man.
She wants not children, that is evident,
for only law-abiding women can give birth
to righteous offspring."

"Queen,
for such you seem to be,
my name is Atalanta of the town of Tegea.
If my hunting dress offends you I am sorry.
But I am unaware of breaking any law
and disagree with you about my offspring.
If I should wed, and may it never come about!
I should be sure to bear far braver, stronger children
than some weaving wife who stays indoors,
for righteous, surely, are the children of a mother
who herself endures a strenuous mode of life."

Silence. Saliva dribbled steadily from the corners of her mouth as I stared into her eyes. The pupils dilated in the gathering gloom. The irises, near black in the sun, turned blue in shadow, even a brilliant purple, except it was not their color I saw but the transparency of her eyes. Looking at them, I felt I was looking into palaces; gates would open, one by one, until I could see into another room. I counted blue rooms and red rooms and entered them as my eyes traveled toward her center, slipping and melting finally into an underworld radiant with new energies, a demonic world of strangeness and magic beyond the horizon where earth shaded over into myth. It was a strange new flashing consciousness for me. At the same time it was clear that I had experienced it before, perhaps in my infancy; certain events connected with the distant past seemed to tremble at the threshold of my memory; I almost touched them, but then they sank back into the depths of my mind like fish leaping out of the water and disappearing into it again before I could do more than glimpse them. (But how can there be any secrets, when we are all the same organism? How can there be any secrecy, when everything is known to all of us?)

Eight

5 Maria Theresienstrasse

19 April

This morning a letter arrived from Cranes. Scanning the nervous florid handwriting on the large lined envelope, I ripped it open to lay bare the great invitation card; Dr. Freud is invited to a "bird shoot" and he and Mrs. Freud to the banquet preceding.

Propping it against my inkwell, I read it through again with an expression of fugitive reproach. In my mind's eye I imagined dozens of carriages and scores of splendid-throated young fellows on horseback. Perhaps even an imperial liege-count or two.

Why do I feel such an incoherent relief at being included, relief that somehow trembles on the edge of indignation? Will it be a new point of departure for me or a return to the starting point?

Gun? Boots?

Coca?

---

24 April

With H on the south side of the river, several miles away.

The place was so deserted, so hidden, with the spreading trees above making for such darkness, and his face was so hot and there was such a sound of wild laughter beneath his words as his eyes passed into mine, filling them as the lightning fills a cloud at sunset. When he kissed me I felt pierced with the piercing thrills of something sharp, sharper even than the thrills of tenderness. I suppose it's lust; it's holy like lightning and the wind. Anyway, I took a sudden loathing to the place and had to leave. H caught at me but I struck out at him and rushed off down the path, sobbing, running from tree to tree, worshipping the forest, the holiness of sunlight, leaves, and grass. I kept on running until my legs died and my chest screamed and pain and fear engulfed me and I fell into some brush and hid myself.

Oh, why are men made as they are? Why are they made as they are? What's the matter with me that I shrink from them? Do other females feel what I feel? Is there some secret conspiracy among us to be silent about this loathing of skin to skin, this disgust of the way men are when they have their will of us? Do I betray some tragic silence that Religion from the beginning has imposed in dark whispers upon her daughters?

Slowly the trembling of my body slowed; slowly I began to

feel once more those long rhythms of the earth that carry one's life. Gradually the sounds of morning gave place to the sounds of afternoon. A beetle crawled toward my hand, climbed over it, dropped off again into the weeds. Out of the corner of my eye I saw a small bird's nest made of green moss and gray lichen. Its fragile valiance astounded me. A wave of gentle softness passed over me as the clarifying power of the forest slowly pushed the world into meaning.

—+—

27 April

Three additional references to Meleager; the last two are alike in identifying him with Hercules, and both introduce additional sons of Thestius.

Hyginus (64 B.C.–A.D. 17)

Oeneus and Ares both slept one night with Althaea, daughter of Thestius. When Meleager was born from them, suddenly in the palace the Fates—Clotho, Lachesis, and Atropos—appeared. They thus sang Meleager's fate: Clotho said that he would be noble, Lachesis said that he would be brave, but Atropos looked at a brand burning on the hearth and said, "He will live as long as that brand remains unconsumed."

Althaea leapt from her bed and doused the fatal brand in water. Later she buried it in the midst of the palace, so that it shouldn't be destroyed by fire.

Apollonius of Rhodes (295–215 *B.C.*)

After them, from Calydon, came the son of Oeneus, strong Meleagros loved of Ares, and Laocoön—Laocoön the brother of Oeneus, though not by the same mother, for a serving-woman bore him—him, now growing old, Oeneus sent to guard his son. Thus Meleagros, still a youth, entered the bold band of heroes.

No other had come superior to Meleagros, I ween—except Hercules—if for one year more he had tarried and been nurtured among the Aetolians. Yea, and his uncle well skilled to fight whether with the javelin or hand to hand, Iphiclus, son of Thestius, bore him company on his way.

Bacchylides (505–450 *B.C.*)

"Hard is it for mortals to bend the resolution of the gods," the shade of Meleager said to Hercules. "Else had car-borne Oeneus allayed the ire of high, flower-crowned, white-armed Artemis, supplicating, fond fire, with sacrifices of many goats and many tawny-hided oxen. But unappeasable was the wrath of the goddess. She sent, huntress maiden, a monster boar of undaunted fierceness into the lovely dales of Calydon; where, resistless in its might, it felled orchards with its tusks, slaughtered fleecy flocks and every mortal it encountered. With it we, picked band of Hellas, waged desperate battle for six days without stay, and when high heaven gave us victory, we set ourselves to bury those whom the tusked monster had slain in furious onset, Ancaeus and Agelaus, best of my dear brothers born of Althaea in the far-famed halls of Oeneus.

"But still more warriors were doomed to fall, for the offended huntress daughter of Latona had not yet ceased her wrath, and we joined fierce battle for the boar's prickly hide. There among many others I slew Iphiclus and good Aphareus, my mother's gallant brethren. For fierce Ares makes no distinction of friend or foe, but shafts fly blindly at opposing ranks, carrying death wherever fortune wills. The sore-stricken daughter of Thestius remembered not this, and—ah, hapless mother—resolved my death—ah, passion-governed woman. She dragged from rich-carved casket and kindled the quickly burning brand that, at my birth, fate doomed to be coeval with my days. At the moment I was stripping of his arms the valiant son of Deipylus, a youth of noble build, whom I had overtaken outside the walls, a sudden faintness seized my soul; I felt my strength decline, alas; and with latest breath wept to feel life's youthful splendor flitting."

Men say the eye of Hercules then and never else was moistened by pity, as thus he answered the ill-starred Meleager's shade: "Mortal's best fate is never to be born, nor ever to behold the sun's bright rays. But nought avails repining: so let my tongue frame words to mold the future. Remains there in the palace of Oeneus, dear to Ares, any virgin daughter of features like to thine? Her would I gladly make my honored bride."

Meleager's shade made answer: "In her father's house I left the sweet-voiced Deinaira, unacquainted yet with mortal-charming, golden Aphrodite."

N.B. Was Deinaira "beloved of Artemis," like Atalanta? If so, why were men like Hercules and Meleager so attracted to Artemisian women?

Obviously the charred brand's a penis symbol; the mother has been given divine power over the son's sexuality, but why?

What was Meleager's root crime? That he was in love with a woman dedicated to the hunt and to virginity, who modeled herself on men and denied the responsibilities of women (children, the hearth, spinning and weaving)? Or was it simply that Atalanta was a stranger, an outsider, a woman from matrilinear Arcadia—too far from the family and social system of Calydon?

What am I learning with this case? Is the Minoan-Mycenaean myth of Atalanta (here dumped into that of Meleager and Hercules) saying that some (which?) of the collection of modes of behavior called "masculine" and "feminine" are entirely alien to healthy men and women, foisted on them by the nature and content of the neuroses? Are Althaea and Oeneus in similar relation to Meleager and Atalanta?

Perhaps it's time to admit (to whom? Breuer? Martha? Sophia?) that my mind is partly lived by unknown, uncontrollable powers, that I am not always aware of how close a relationship exists between my research and my subjective emotional need. If I can fight my way through to a coherent organization of mental processes—a sort of metapsychological view of mental life—perhaps I'll be able to emancipate myself from some of my inherited symptoms of consciousness, symptoms passed on through the distant ages, grounded in the childhood of humanity and existing now as a collective mind that undergoes mental processes as though it were an individual— ?

No. I've lost it.

When you want to understand something you stand in front of it, alone, without help; all the past in the world is of no use. Then it disappears and what you wanted to understand disappears with it.

Cranes

2 May

At Cranes the great hall was brilliantly lit. Dozens of
Meissen lamps cast circles of opaque yellow light, a kind of
tarnished gold, over the company, and there were flickering
sidelights from log fires burning brightly at both ends. As
Martha and I entered I looked at myself in one of the mirrors.
I am handsome, I said to myself. I have deep, dark eyes and
glossy hair. My bearing is elegant without being in any way
arrogant.

In the middle of the room was a piece of furniture so large
my eye must have rejected it on previous visits: a twelve-legged
Carolean banqueting board, at least twenty-five feet long,
gleaming, heavily carved, laden with food. To one side of this
Herr O was standing beneath a large oil painting depicting
trees and birds and bunches of fruit. As I watched his eyes find
mine, I felt a sense of taboo, as if eating and drinking with this
man were forbidden, as if the path I am treading on with him
and his daughter will sooner or later lead to terrible secrets
about myself as well as them.

"Mrs. Freud . . . charming. And Dr. Freud, you're just in
time. I was hoping for the chance to ask you about the term
'psychotic.' Applied to myself, for instance, would it imply a
few facial tics—or perhaps a stammer?"

I smiled at the group surrounding him. "Definitely a stammer, yes."

"But perhaps I am merely neurotic. How would you define
the neuroses?"

"The neuroses are various forms and degrees of the impairment of happiness and the capacity to work that plague one's friends but never oneself."

He laughed richly.

"And normalcy, Dr. Freud? How would you define that?"

He paused for a moment to let us admire the craftsmanship of his being, each shift of energy a calculation. Then he continued. "Let me tell you what disturbs me about psychology. Your so-called psyche-logos, or science of the soul, terms great elation a state of hypomanic disturbance, as though it were a hilarious distress. Charcot and others have made it quite clear that all high degrees of intensification, whether of chastity or sensuality, of scruples or negligence, of cruelty or compassion, in the long run end up as something pathological."

"Not at all," I said to him. "You have misinterpreted our fledgling science. Let me assure you that bourgeois sexual morality, for instance—as society in its most extreme form, the Americans, defines it—seems to me very contemptible. Although hermaphroditism, homosexuality, pedophilia, sodomy, fetishism, coprophilia, and necrophilia are perversions, they are accomplishing a piece of mental work with remarkable success."

"Really? You astound me, Doctor."

"Indeed," I continued, "the omnipotence of love shows itself perhaps nowhere more strongly than in such aberrations as these."

"Am I to take it, then, that you approve of deviations from the normal sexual object and the normal sexual aim?"

"I approve of facts. All human beings are innately perverse. Neurotics, whose symptoms form a kind of negative counterpart to the perversions, only display this universal primitive disposition more emphatically than so-called normal people."

"That's my point, Freud. Why cure them? How meaningless healthy life would be if it had no other goal than a medial state between two extremes. Consider sadism, a perversion you did not mention. We hear it is the personality characteristic of the individual who can achieve sexual gratification only by forcing his sexual partner to experience extreme suffering. But this alleged perversion is actually no more disconnected from normal human behavior than overeating is from eating. The sadist dominates his partner; so does any normal man. Masculinity is the attitude of demand toward one's circumstances, the ability to dominate the social and physical environment. It is the power to adjust one's strategies so that the environment contributes to one's desire to live."

"And femininity, Joachim?" asked Sophia. Her voice was silken as she approached our little group and smiled at Martha. "I am so curious as to how you would define femininity."

(At this point I had to flinch from asking myself whether I felt jealous and of whom. Why does this strange foreign woman's body seem to glow with power? Why am I so susceptible to her elusive, shifty, soul-shattering confidence? Have I fallen in love with her? Is there some voluptuous flame permanently aglow in her supple spine?)

Herr O spread his hands. "Sophiamou, it's really quite simple. Femininity is the power to recognize the limitations of one's will, to accept those elements that cannot be changed, and to cooperate with the unchanging conditions of the environment, particularly social conditions."

"I see. And does this power always involve suffering?"

"To be whipped in sexual circumstances is to have one's strategy of acceptance confirmed. The gratification involved comes from the reinforcement of what might as well be called a faith."

"And the blood of innocent creatures?"

"Ah . . . you do not approve of our coming sport, I fear."

"It is not my idea of sport; it is my idea of hatred and murder. For every hero does there have to be a living sacrifice? Do you always need death to complete your pleasure?"

There was a pause, and then Herr O told an elaborate joke about some soldiers hunting in the Black Forest. Much later in the evening he came to my side.

"How is our Lucy progressing? Do you understand what's wrong with her?"

"Well . . . I prefer to speak in general, of hysterical patients in general . . . since I am still working toward a general theory of hysteria based on notions drawn from my reading, my patients, my self-knowledge."

"I have to know one thing, Freud. Did she say I took advantage of her?"

"I . . . uh . . ."

"Did she say that I would kiss her feet?"

"I don't think—"

"You might as well tell me the truth, Freud. Did she picture me on my knees begging her to forgive me? Did she?"

"Really, sir. I can't allow—"

"She is lying. Lying! You know, old boy, I would never permit myself to make an anti-Semitic remark; but I will observe that it takes a Jew to go all the way to Paris to discover a practice—mesmerism—that everyone else has long since abandoned. My daughter will never be cured! She'll just get worse! Because with her illness she holds *me* responsible for the death of her mother. She is getting revenge, punishing *me*, making *me* pay for what hurt *me* the most, the death of her mother. As if that death wasn't enough for *me* to bear all my life . . ."

He went on ranting for several minutes. Slipping into the role of son, which he was determined to force on me, I affected hearty good humor and took advantage of the atmosphere and situation to make the most insulting remarks, which produced exactly the desired effect. He whined and whimpered and pretended not to understand me, but he was helpless against my psychological frankness.

I told him there were many lessons in life he hadn't learned because he was too well off to bother—that he was essentially a brute, a retarded guttersnipe—that his friendliness was pure pretense, obviously he was itching for attention, affection, etc. I had a fiendishly good time. I couldn't get enough. My final summing up: wolf in sheep's clothing, liar, swindler, hypocrite, braggart (murderer?).

3 May

    I stood transfixed on the balmy edge of night and stared at my celestial visitant as if I had never before seen the moon under any sky. How does it make me feel? Is there something about it that every woman who has ever lived must feel? Something that even men have been comforted by?

O my moon, last remaining fragment of some earlier stellar system, nearer in your origins to the beginning of things, your whiteness is inextinguishable, your whiteness beyond all whiteness, your whiteness like the wet curves of seashells, like the spray about the prows of ships.

Bury, oh, bury your strange secret in my breast! Bury it deep, deep in my womb, so that henceforth to the end of my days, something cold and free and uncaught may make me strong!

⇥

3 May

On the eve of the bird shoot I lay in troubled sleep among the luxuriant growths of my own fantasies, dense as a tropical vegetation. From time to time I woke to half-remember a dream or the boom of violent thunder. In the morning I felt immeasurably aged, yet at one and the same time as new to the world as a foetus hanging from the birth cord.

I breakfasted and left for Cranes. To the east the sky was covered with clouds. As I entered the park, a thunderstorm broke over the entire valley, throwing down a strange radiance. Flights of glittering needles pocked the gray waters of the river. As usual, when I heard the thunder, I registered the complex of associated ideas linking storms with thoughts of parental and divine anger, guilt, primitive fear, etc.

I joined a party of other hunters (they greeted me cheerfully enough) and marched defiantly about in a forest of my own heartbeats, making as much noise as possible with my boots, shouting at the dogs, cracking my whip, and so forth.

Everyone seemed to have all the impedimenta of professional hunters: gun cases, cartridge bags, binoculars, flasks. Together we entered the penumbra of the storm slowly, marveling at the light, at the horizon drawn back like a bow. There was something timeless and ancient in the scene. I felt a pervading stoic melancholy under the rain as we crossed the water meadows west of the house. The brilliant unfamiliar lighting seemed to recreate the world, giving everything a spectral, storybook air. Faint gleams of light suggested the gun flashes of distant ships in a naval engagement.

Gradually a sense of unreality overtook me. I had the feeling of two dreams overlapping, one displacing the other. I felt as one does in particularly intense dreams when one walks without touching the ground, or rises deliberately through the air like a cork through water.

Then everything started clearing. It was as if a curtain were being drawn aside to reveal . . . Herr O in his element, his gestures brisk with wood fires and roving gundogs. Under the trees, servants began unpacking hampers of food, and on the grass they set up folding tables and chairs. Everyone feasted on lobster vol-au-vents, chicken mayonnaise, champagne. The weather was rapidly clearing, the marsh-mist full of evanescent shapes and contours. The whole surface of the river was rising into the sky like the floor of a theater, pouring upward with the mist.

Afternoon: After lunch, as I approached the house to see Lucy, the shooting was starting up again in the water meadows; little puffs of smoke were just visible above the trees.

In her room, I saw at once that she was extremely agitated.

When she saw me, her eyes darted up like birds flying off a branch.

"My mother! My mother!"

"You are remembering your mother?"

"Her body is in the earth and turned to dust! Her soul is up there where the stars and angels are, but what is that to me? I am here—am I not?"

Hypnosis:

The hunt begins.
The royal party comes upon
a sunken immemorial marsh.
Pale light glimmers here.
Willows sway among the reeds.
At a signal from Meleager all dismount
but boxer Castor and his brother Pollux.
These two, staying on horseback,
ride off to flush the beast into the day.
Meleager talks to Telamon.
Atalanta spreads her nets and grooms her dogs.
The progeny of Artemis enters and is ominously still.
Not liking to at first,
but gaining strength from their considerable number,
the hunters shout and wave their bows and spears.
The beast attacks,
trampling trees and scattering dogs
with deadly sidelong strokes of its enormous tusks.
Eurytion is the first to cast a spear—into a willow tree.
The next to cast is Plexippus, Meleager's uncle,
whose shaft is overthrown with too much need of praise

and arcs above the monster's back to pin a yelping dog.
Ancaeus lifts his axe; the boar rushes underneath
and spills his groin and stomach on the ground.
Mad with blood, the creature charges at will.
Androgeus is gored behind the knees
and with his sinews gone, dies.
Ares sheds violent night on Androgeus' eyes.
In the intense confusion
all have lost their heads except for one.
Unbidden, her hounds leap from her side.
Emboldened, her arrow penetrates the monster's flank
but Artemis' indomitable boar remains alive.
A spear is tossed by Toxeus
that veers and slays the beautiful Alexias.
Jason casts, misses.
At last Meleager,
son and heir of Oeneus and Althaea,
rooted to the ground with gathered concentration,
bares his ashwood pole and throws it to the creature's back.
With godlike speed he rushes forward with a second spear
and plunges it between the monster's eyes.
It is the killing blow.
The boar of Calydon lies dead upon the earth.

Afterward I gave her a mild sedative, woke her up, and rejoined the hunters. There was time to reflect that Atalanta seems rather shadowy in this part of the poem. If this is the ur-myth, why doesn't she kill the boar herself? Perhaps Lucy, even under hypnotism, is keeping things from me? Walking down-river, I approached the woods and heard Herr O's beaters coming closer through the undergrowth, walking deliberately through the thickets, tapping the tree trunks with their sticks, emitting a mixture of low-pitched churring, whistling, and whooping sounds. I decided to join them and started hooting and crying, frightening small birds, which scattered with alarm calls through the bushes. Then the gulls began to call, then the first shots—then suddenly they all seemed to break, hundreds and thousands of birds flying out over the guns and all the guns firing at once, each with two loaders, one to receive the empty gun, one to hand it back reloaded, while the shooter himself never moved his gaze from the oncoming birds. For several hours the air was full of gunfire, falling birds, the smell of cordite, the thump of bodies on the ground.

Afterward I watched as the men who had been shooting relaxed and strolled toward each other, their hands in their pockets or lighting cigars. As the dogs went about their work of retrieving the fallen birds, the gold of late afternoon was succeeded by the pinkish gray of early evening. I was still there when the game cart drew near to receive its final burden of the day. Drawn by an old cart-horse, it moved off down the drive toward Cranes, whose chimneys could be seen among the trees some distance away. The loaders and dog handlers followed, while the rest of the beaters and gamekeepers dispersed in the general direction of the front gate.

I turned to leave, but saw several hunters standing around something that had fallen on the ground. I approached and saw to my horror that Herr O had been shot. "An accident," someone said. He was lying underneath a tree with his neck supported by it, at an angle that cocked his head forward, so that he appeared to be studying the wounds in his own body. His eyes alone were moving, but they could only reach up to the knees of his onlookers. Pain had changed them from their normal periwinkle blue to the dull blue of seawater or plumbago.

I crouched and stared at him, reproving my own curiosity, the interest, even elation, with which a large part of my professional mind always responds to human tragedy (it never seems to me that I have a right to be so interested). His legs, for instance. His legs were not a man's legs, neither the stalwart muscular ones nor the lean sinewy ones, but those of a girl, a not very good-looking girl with gentle plain legs.

"I want to see my daughter," he said.

In the next half-hour the place became full of servants; the air became dark with their concern. Sophia arrived with Lucy, pale and tempestuously calm. Herr O ground his teeth. He groaned as they lifted him to look at her. Lucy knelt. It was a matter of minutes, of seconds. She took his dangling hand and kissed it. "Oh," she said, furiously clasping and unclasping the hand and moving from one knee to the other in an ecstasy of horror and dreadful excitement, "if only I could make you see."

He was dead. Sophia and Lucy and most of the servants went back to the house. Stillness settled down over the scene. No one seemed to know what to do next. There were whispered consultations. At last the body was carried toward the house. In twos and threes, in silent constraint, the hunters went back to their rooms.

In the great hall, when I arrived, it was apparent the company had heard there was something amiss. Many of the women had changed into traveling clothes. In the dining room, dinner had begun, but in an atmosphere of confusion; guests were eating in haste, like travelers with no time to lose. There was a continuous coming and going up and down stairs, a back-and-forth between the dining room and the bedrooms upstairs. Those who had finished their meal and finished packing stood about exchanging goodbyes. And that was how the day ended. Baskets and boxes and cases were collected, capes and blankets folded and stacked. One by one the carriages drove away, laden with bundles and passengers. By evening, the mist was rising again from the ground, still low but thickening, beginning to spread a layer of damp haze which in the morning would linger on the grass like spilt milk, while the sky above it became the pale clear blue of another day.

The Golden
Age

Nine

The funeral was this afternoon. Martha and I arrived with the Breuers, joining the growing stream of carriages from the houses in the vicinity, gaping at the huge black flag that had been hung from the gable of the house and almost reached down to the drive. To the side of the front door, wearing black silk with a cape and veil, Sophia stood with Lucy's two uncles, Herr O's brothers, greeting the visitors and doing the honors.

We entered the big drawing room and I smelled the heavy perfume of the flowers and wreaths. For some reason the coffin had been laid in here in the place usually occupied by the piano. Herr O in his coffin, decked with all his flowers, had been introduced to Cranes like a new piece of furniture.

It was like a release and a piece of good fortune when, stepping nearer, I saw that the lid of the coffin was closed. My patient of almost a year was beside it, her skin seeming transparent, her hand from time to time touching the wood. Several of the visitors remarked at her calmness, indeed admired her; her calmness was due to the morphine I had given her earlier.

10 May

A consulting physician was brought in by the family—a Dr. R, whom I have met. For over half an hour Lucy couldn't see him; it was a genuine negative hallucination. He succeeded in breaking through it only by blowing smoke in her face. Suddenly she saw a stranger before her, rushed to the door to take away the key that must have let the stranger in, and crumpled to the floor. When she tried to get up, the whole right side of her body seemed to slip sideways. Her head drooped and wobbled to and fro as if it were about to drop off. She was deathly pale.

Dr. R knelt by her side; she gripped his hands (his hands were small, pampered, beautiful). She said to him, "I saw my father on his deathbed. Abandoned by everybody. Like a dog. He had a death's head."

"A death's head?" said Dr. R.

"Yes. Like skeletons. It must have been a mask. They put them on dead bodies, don't they?"

"It must have been painful for you."

"Very painful," Lucy agreed. "If only I could see his fingers, those great fingers of his that I loved. If only I could take his hands, his big hands that I loved. He used to take me in his strong hands and lift me off the ground . . . Leave me alone! Leave me alone!" She started tearing her hair.

I said to the consulting physician, "We mustn't overtax her. You had better withdraw now. We won't get anything else out of her. I'll try and sort this out."

In the evening a violent outburst of excitement was succeeded by a profound stupor, from which she emerged greatly changed. She exhibited hysterical contractions of the muscles around the spine and other new symptoms. Strong suicidal impulses appeared, which made it seem inadvisable for her to continue living on the second floor.

11 May

We have moved her to one of the reception rooms on the ground floor. She stares out the window, immobile.

12 May

The O brothers have departed for their estates. (Why is it only when alone that I am able to participate fully? Why is it only after people have gone that I am able to take them into myself, the more deeply the farther away they go?)

17 May

The days pass in silence. I am seeing Lucy six days a week, excluding only Sundays. Nothing happens. I can neither write nor concentrate my thoughts. I spend leisure hours of extreme boredom turning from one thing to another, cutting open books, looking at maps, playing patience or chess, unable to continue at anything for long.

20 May

Sophia has gone to Berlin, where Herr Schliemann's ear condition has taken a turn for the worse.

I'm at the end of my tether!

21 May

"I'm not going to the Breuers' for dinner, Martha."

"Don't be crazy! You adore them. It's only with them that you feel comfortable."

"When they're alone, yes. But they've invited some idiot along too."

"Who?"

"Some Dr. Fliess, whom I've never met."

"If you've never met him, then how do you know he's an idiot?"

"Because he has come from Berlin to attend my lectures at the institute."

"Really?"

"Yes, can you imagine? A Berlin doctor, a man of my own age, and apparently very successful there."

"Well, then?"

"I shall teach him nothing. Nothing! I'm a failure, I have nothing to teach anybody, look at what I have done to Lucy."

"What do you mean?"

"This morning, when I tried to put her to sleep, I completely failed to bring about hypnosis. 'I'm not asleep,' she said to me in a funny, horrid way. 'I can't be hypnotized anymore.' "

"What did you do?"

"She was in open rebellion. The situation was very grave. I gave up trying to hypnotize her and announced that I would give her forty-eight hours to think things over. That's where the matter rests!"

"Oh, dear . . ."

"A fight is being waged inside her, Martha—night and day. I must start again . . . An incomplete story under hypnosis produces no therapeutic—"

"Incomplete story?"

"I'm determined to search for a new method with her. Perhaps it will be possible to use hypnosis in a quite different manner. I don't know. That's just the trouble, I know nothing—and meanwhile Breuer is singing my praises to this—this—"

"If this Dr. Fliess has come because of you, that's an extra reason for going to the dinner."

"Martha! You don't understand! Talking to you, talking to

her! Writing up entries in a case history! Not a penny to my name! I'm going to give up medicine! I might just as well sell cloth like my father!"

"Oh, Sigi." She was, finally, in tears. "You promised me you'd be happy."

"Happy?"

"Yes . . . so long as we'd be living together."

"My poor love, I'm spoiling your life. I should never have married you. Forgive me, Martha."

At the Breuers':

Already this Fliess intrigues and captivates me; I feel toward him a gentleness and a desire to please hitherto reserved for Breuer and Charcot. In his long thin body, which could be graceful, there's a kind of Prussian stiffness. His movements have a strong mechanical precision that belies the high starched collar, four-in-hand tie, fancy waistcoat, etc. With his imperious gaze and inscrutable countenance—his awesome, dignified bearing—he's really an extraordinary male presence.

"I can't understand," I said to him, "why a man of your worth, a Berlin specialist, should have gone out of his way just to hear my lectures. I'm not even a professor!"

"If I've come to you, Freud, it's because your reputation has come to me."

"But I only teach anatomy of the brain. Others do it as well or better."

"You know that's not true! The old fossils in power divide the brain up into thousands of little compartments, each of which supposedly corresponds to one of our gestures, one of our sensations, one of our ideas, and so forth. You're one of the few men in Europe to teach that those compartments don't exist, that everything's a matter of connections and movement."

I bowed my head to conceal an almost indecent smile of satisfaction.

"Perhaps Breuer has told you," he continued, "I'm an ear-nose-and-throat man. I'll tell you a little secret, Freud. I've managed to isolate a neurosis. The nasal neurosis, if you like." He placed his hand on my shoulder in a comradely way. "I could go further if I had a more thorough knowledge of neurology."

"Further in what way?"

"There's a nervous connection between the nose and all the other organs; I'm certain of it. By numbing the nasal region I've actually caused intestinal disturbances to disappear."

He was speaking with a burning, barely suppressed enthusiasm. I stared at his black-dilated, spellbound eyes. According to Mathilde Breuer ("She filled my ears with him," Martha told me later), everyone in Berlin admires his captivating personality, his wealthy, accomplished wife, Ida, etc. He is educated in the humanities and makes allusions to both classical and modern literature. Best of all, he pronounces himself interested in the possible effects of applying cocaine to the nasal membranes, the nose's relation to sexuality, etc.

After dinner (turbot) I cornered him and made a little speech. "How fortunate I would feel to find a friend and esteemed colleague in one person, Dr. Fliess. Although our meeting has been occasioned by professional matters, I must confess I have hopes of continuing the intercourse with you on a friendly basis—"

I broke the cigar that I had been bringing up to my mouth.

"You know, you smoke too much, Freud." He seemed very serious.

"You're quite right."

"You should at least give up the late evening cigars. They are terrible." I hesitated, felt a wave of submission, and threw the ruined cigar into the fireplace. Breuer came up and said to Fliess, "Bravo! For three years I've been trying to convince him, and you succeed at the first try."

Even Martha felt called upon to comment. "He doesn't dare smoke in front of you, Dr. Fliess. If only you could use your influence to stop him completely!" To which Fliess replied, "I shall forbid him tobacco, madam, only when I am certain of being obeyed."

I foresee a passionate friendship, perhaps the first of my life. Is it possible he'll even understand that my deprecation of my capacities springs not from an inner weakness but from a terrifying strength, one I feel unable to cope with alone?

Toward the end of the long evening (I had taken a bit of cocaine) there came a downpour with thunder and lightning. Fliess left precipitately, running into the night without even his hat. Shortly afterward, as Martha and I were taking our leave (let me try to describe exactly what happened), there was a great clap of noise close at hand, the sound and the flash together; then, there before us, on a rocky slab just outside Breuer's door, all gleaming and glittering in the night blue light, was a tall naked man somewhat similar to Fliess in physiognomy but much taller, with dripping hair and beard and a ribbon of seaweed on his shoulder.

"How absurd!" I wanted to shout at him, but he had disappeared around the side of the house.

Because she was looking the other way, Martha had missed him completely.

23 May

Something rather odd and distressing has just occurred. After seeing Lucy (the contractions are less severe; she speaks about whatever enters her mind; no hypnosis), I decided, as the weather was fine, to walk over to the Cranes lake and sit on a rock looking out over the water. The sun was shining and there was very little wind; I thought how the water glowed rather than sparkled in the bland sunshine. Then, not at once but after about two minutes, as my eyes became accustomed to the glare, I saw a kind of monster rising from the water in the middle of the lake. At first it looked like a black snake breaking the surface and arching itself upward: I could see the head with remarkable clarity, a kind of crested snake's head, green-eyed, the mouth opening to show teeth and a pink interior. There followed an elongated neck and a long thickening body with a ridgy spiny back. At the end was something that might have been a flipper or perhaps a fin. Then the whole thing collapsed, the fin disappeared, the undulating back broke the water, and there was nothing but a great foaming swirling pool where the creature had vanished.

The shock and horror of it were so great that for some time I could not move. I wanted to run—fearing beyond anything that the animal would reappear closer to land, perhaps rising up at my very feet—but my legs would not function and my heart was beating so violently that any exertion might have rendered me unconscious. So I sat there. The water became calm and nothing further happened. In the carriage taking me home, I leaned my head against my hands for fifteen minutes before I was able to write down what appears as this entry.

—◁—

23 May

   Silence. Cut off from hearing, cut off from sound. (At least I am immune from sanity and insanity.)

   What a senseless degrading havoc I have made of my poor sweet human life!

24 May

   What torments me most of all is that now I can never give my father the love he deserves, never repay him for his concern, his kindness.

—◁—

25 May

   As soon as I entered my study after lunch I was aware that something had happened, though I could not understand what. Then I realized that my terra-cotta Isis was gone from its pedestal. It had fallen onto the floor and was broken into a great many pieces. How? Why? The pedestal is perfectly steady and has not moved. There has been no wind, the curtain is motionless, the maid is forbidden entry to this room.

Perhaps I shifted the vase very slightly when I dusted it a few days ago? Or has there been an earth tremor?

I am reluctant to think that I am to blame, and I am sure I am not. But how can the statue have jumped off its stand?

I picked up the pieces and put them in a drawer.

27 May

As she returns to life, something dogmatic and imperious in her reminds me of her father. This morning, when I asked her again about hypnosis, she said in an obstinate, defiant manner reminiscent of Herr O; "I-can-tell-you-in-advance-that-it-would-turn-out-badly-because-it-is-contrary-to-my-nature-and-it-was-the-same-with-my-father."

Why is she identifying with him in this way? Is it a form of regression or sexual confusion? Or could it make sense that an adolescent girl, after she has had to relinquish her father as love object, would bring her masculinity into prominence and identify herself with her father (that is, with the object that has been lost) instead of her mother?

Hypothesis: Lucy wanted to reject her father's sexual advances but felt tremendous fear. Where was this fear to go? Her personality was insufficiently consolidated for her to be able to protest, so she forgot herself entirely and identified totally with the aggressor. It was an identification based on fear, and the most important transformation in the emotional life of the child that it called forth was the introjection of the guilt feeling of the adult. It was nothing less than the premature grafting of passionate sexual love riddled with guilt onto a still immature, innocent being. (And perhaps her body in the end, against her own will, betrayed her to him every time? There are undeniable manifestations of sexual passions in childhood, though an uncannily effective forgetfulness, an undefeatable amnesia, seems to cover the earliest years like a heavy blanket.)

3 June

She agreed to tell me a dream.

She was leaving a sanatorium for nervous diseases with whose "doctor/director" she had been in love. This doctor/director appeared at the train station and handed her a bouquet of flowers as a parting present. It was rather awkward because her father was there to witness the tribute.

So! I am replacing her father in her imagination! *She* is not just identifying with him, she is identifying *me* with him as well, *transferring* to me feelings that she once had for her father. The precondition must be that she doesn't remember anything of her original emotions toward her father because she's forgotten and repressed them, but she acts them out. She reproduces them not as a memory but as an action, and she repeats the action without, of course, knowing that she is repeating it. She does not say that she remembers that she used to be defiant and critical toward her father's authority; instead, she behaves in that way to *me*, her doctor!

I am tempted to say to her, "It is from Herr O that you

have made a transference onto me. Have you been struck by anything about me or got to know anything about me that has caught your fancy, as happened previously with your father? Is there some detail in our relation, or in my person or circumstance, that reminds you of him?"

(What could it be, the unknown quantity in me that reminds her of Herr O?)

5 June

She dreamed about a girl who walked through a tunnel and entered a large open storybook, where she came upon a marble statue of a bird. "The girl fell asleep, and when she woke up she was leaning against the base of the statue. Her forehead had struck something and was bleeding."

Apparently the girl was totally absorbed in bird studies. She had turned completely away from life and its pleasures; sculpted marble and bronze alone were truly alive for her; they alone expressed the purpose and value of human life.

Is this pointing me somewhere? Toward psychological methodology in dreams? Could dream events actually be assessed as legitimate mental events?

Science would answer no: it explains dreaming as a purely physiological process, behind which, accordingly, there is no need to look for sense, meaning, or purpose. Somatic stimuli, so it says, play upon the mental instrument during sleep and bring to consciousness now one idea and now another, robbed of all mental content. Dreams are comparable only to twitchings, not to expressive movements, of the mind.

But it seems to me this flies in the face of everyday experience that people's thoughts and feelings are continued in their sleep. And Lucy's statue is of a bird! Among the ancients the study of birds (their flight, their notes, their habits, their migrations) was incessant. To them a bird was *always* an omen, always ominous. Birds came and went where man and beast could not—up to the sun, high among the rainclouds. Since they were so near the heavenly signs, they must keep their sanctity longer than other living creatures, they must know more than men—

And beneath this Greco-Roman notion of birds as portents lies an earlier stratum of thought (Pelasgian? Egyptian?) in which birds are regarded not merely as portents of the weather but as potencies who actually *make* it—not, that is, as messengers but as magicians—

However. Do I really venture, in the face of the reproaches of strict Science, to become a partisan of antiquity and superstition? Nowadays, in Europe at least, only the "common people," who cling to superstitions and who in this regard are carrying on the convictions of antiquity, continue to insist that dreams can be interpreted.

6 June

"How is Lucy?"

"Yes, Martha?"

"Is your new method working with her?"

"We must wait and see."

"How do Fleischl's books help?"

"We shall see, we shall see."

"I don't like that Fliess of yours, you know."

"Why not?"

"He doesn't like Breuer. It's obvious."

"Why do you change the subject?"

"That Fliess. He frightens me. You're like a little boy in front of him."

"True enough, Martha. Like a little boy."

"I wonder what you find in him."

"He's an adventurer."

"And you approve of that?"

"Yes. No adventurers, no science. The world belongs to them. Perhaps he'll give me the strength to become one."

She rose and began pacing irritably up and down.

"Come sit down for a bit, Martha. Come sit here next to me."

She smiled faintly and sat down on the arm of my chair. "Well?"

"Well. You've seen him. He's a man."

"And Breuer isn't one?"

"Breuer's a Viennese. Intelligent, subtle, but skeptical. Fliess, he's a Prussian."

"He certainly does look like one. Stiff as a poker."

"Stiff and hard. A soldier. You've seen his eyes."

"Yes."

"I've never seen handsomer ones. He's the one you should have married."

"What a dreadful idea!"

"You'd have had a virile, strong, fascinating husband."

She bent over me, half teasing, half tender, and caressed my beard. "The one I have got fascinates me more than anyone, provided he takes the trouble. And I think his eyes are the handsomest in the world. Once he deigns to look Fliess in the face, Fliess' great eyes will shatter like glass!"

—✦—

7 June

Dream: I was in a dark high wood of lofty pines. There were people all about in the shadows, waiting. Then a murmur spread around, carrying fear. "The White Grebe!" "The White Grebe!"

Everyone cowered down into the shadows, waiting in terror. But I could not hide; I knew that something was coming for me. A white bird like a heron circled down from the high trees. I stood with my hands outstretched, holding my heart in the palms of my hands. The white bird settled on my heart and dug its claws in and I realized it was a phoenix, the flaming bird that burns itself to ashes to revive its life.

8 June

After breakfast I went down to the river and followed the stream of green grass flowing beneath the foliage. In the silence I heard a bird—I imagined it to be a nightingale, but how could it be if they only sing at night?—a bird that repeated the same phrase over and over, a sweet greeting that came down through the leaves, an invitation to roam wide through the forest. "O spheral, spheral!" the bird seemed to say; "O holy,

holy! O clear away, clear away! O clear up, clear up!" inter-spersed with the finest trills and the most delicate preludes.

I imagined myself on the brink of a mysterious felicity; a moment later a gull alighted quite close to me, with wings stretched above its back in that fashion peculiar to big-winged birds when they settle on the ground. I felt myself into its movement with a kind of ecstasy. Immediately I had the idea that my awareness had somehow widened, that I was feeling what I saw as well as seeing what I saw. I felt like that gull, but also like the one-celled animal that spreads part of its vital essence to flow round and envelop within itself what it wants for food.

In other words, without thinking, I was automatically mak-ing discoveries about movements that are the same as internal acts of thought. It's an utterly new capacity, more diffuse than deciding or intending, more subtle than anything I've ever tried with running or drawing—more like the spreading of invisible sentient feelers, as a sea anemone spreads wide its feathery fingers . . .

My God! I can send out the streamers of my thought on every side; the beam of my attention is not of fixed width. At any moment there are faint patternings in the fringes of my thoughts which can be brought to distinctness if I look at them. I can survey the whole sky at the same moment if I wish. I can widen or narrow my focus as I choose.

I decided to spread my awareness toward some ilex trees, letting myself flow round them, letting myself feed on the delicacy of their patterns until all their intricacies became part of my being. I felt, "There's a bird singing high in the treetops inside me."

I don't remember the precise gesture that lifted me up, but gradually I began noticing white cottages and lanes and tidy green fields, and something, either the shape or the pattern or the character of the land, aroused such a deep resonance in me that I flew, as if meeting my lover, faster and faster, aglow with an almost unbearable light.

Ten

5 Maria Theresienstrasse

11 June

Fliess came home with me after my lecture on cerebral neurasthenia. He seemed irritable and rather excited. Settling into his
chair, he began to talk.

"We're of a different breed, Freud. We're visionaries. We
have ideas before we possess the means to verify them. There
are hidden powers in us."

"How do you know?"

"A visionary can be recognized immediately."

"By what?"

"By his eyes. Listen to me, Freud. You're the only person
who can help me. I'm close to success. I've seen the truth. I
shall turn biology upside down. My theories are almost com-

plete. What remains is to prove everything. That's the easiest part. Above all, if you give me your help."

"Your praise is nectar and ambrosia to me, Wilhelm."

"Yes, but I need fewer compliments and more facts. Breuer was telling me about your patient, Lucy O. He says she suffered a relapse when her father died . . ."

"A traumatism, in the most literal sense. The timing was execrable! I had been unlocking the . . . nature of the relationship between them."

"You mean . . . sex?"

"Yes. When she was a young child, in my opinion, her father took advantage of her."

"Date of birth?"

"I know it by heart: 15 February 1870."

"Date of the sexual attack?"

"When she was very young."

"Freud, I'm asking you for the day, the month, and the hour."

"Don't be absurd, Wilhelm. It's just a theory until she remembers it."

"How do you expect me to work on such vague data?"

"I don't—"

"Do you know what we need, Freud? An exceptionally talented person, one who could understand our mutual research and assist it."

"But—"

"Come now, how about Lucy?"

"Lucy!"

"Freud, she's an exceptional case. It's obvious from what you and Breuer have said that she can be *useful* to us."

I was astonished. "Be useful to *us!* But what possible connection . . . ?"

"Lucy's a proof of the nasal neurosis and the sexual theory. I *know* it." His voice was harsh. "She must be worked on hard and without respite. Until she delivers up her secrets." He put his hand on my arm. "We have to prepare her, Freud. One can operate only on a healthy body. Now's the time." He spoke like a surgeon. "I'd find it quite unacceptable for her to be lost to science. Do something, Freud. Find a new method."

"I'm not sure Breuer—"

"Find a new method! You have no right to hold back the advance of science just to spare Breuer's susceptibilities."

14 June

The idea occurred to me of touching her, of applying pressure to her head while instructing her to report to me faithfully whatever appeared before her "inner eye" or passed through her memory at the moment of the pressure.

"Lucy, you must say the thing that comes into your head under the pressure of my hands."

"What do you mean?"

"Let me show you." I pressed her temples with my palms. "Well?"

"I only felt dizzy."

"What were you thinking about when you felt dizzy?"

"I wasn't thinking of anything; I only felt dizzy."

"That isn't possible, Lucy. Fugue states like that—dizzy spells—never happen without being accompanied by some idea. I shall press once more, and the thought you had will come back to you."

Determined to elicit the forgotten memory, I placed my hand firmly on her forehead and said, "You will think of it under the pressure of my hand . . . Well, what has occurred to you?"

She remained silent for a long time; then, on my insistence, she admitted she had had thoughts of her father; the touching had reminded her of a similar touching that had happened in her childhood. She couldn't remember any details, but I intend to continue to make use of this technique of bringing out ideas and pictures by means of pressing on the patient's head. (Perhaps there are other "hysterogenic" spots? When you touch them in a certain way you awaken a memory, which triggers further associations, etc.?)

⚊⚌⚊

14 June

When he pressed my forehead he said this gesture would mark the beginning of a new era between us. Oh! There is so much fire and so much love in me! To think that a few months ago I was afraid to be alone in a room with a man other than Father!

Later. I imagined my lover coming behind me, gently caressing my bare shoulders and holding me close. We kissed, his warm hands encircling my breasts; we floated, smooth as tree trunks, smooth as snakes, our twistings strangely black and sleek. We sped through the striped and speckled forest; I heard the soft rustling flight of wings. From me to my lover was only as far as to the next tree. Inscape linked our living beings so we were never apart. Every moment the sunshine grew more golden. There were larkspurs big and grand, long spires of blue delphiniums, flowering cherry and apple trees with pink-and-white buds. I saw a plum tree that had burst open wide in the golden summer air, snow white with blossoms and musical with bees like a fairy king's canopy—and over everything a wild clear scented sweetness of glossy dark green leaves . . .

⊷

16 June

Told that Sophia had returned from Berlin, I canceled Lucy's session, ran to the dairy, and banged on the door. She appeared in a minute or two, wearing a black-and-white traveling costume.

"Sigmund. I've just seen Lucy."

Sophia! "How is your husband?"

"Better, thanks. Apparently the ear condition is from years of bathing in the sea. But Lucy!"

"What about her?"

"She's still very ill—seriously ill."

"Her father died. She is naturally upset."

"What is happening now in the treatment?"

"I . . . she is resisting. She is repressing her memories, even under hypnosis."

" 'She resisted me, so I killed her.' I've forgotten what melodrama that's from."

"Sophia! You couldn't joke if you understood her symptoms. Strong methods are needed now. I need to go down. Plumb the deep recesses."

"But I don't . . . If she's repressing her memories, as you put it, isn't it because they're unbearable for her?"

"Yes, but—"

"Isn't it legitimate for a child of seventeen to want to forget things? Isn't it right for her to bury within herself a memory that frightens her?"

"Sophia! You don't understand! The bullet that killed her father shattered his spine, so for twenty-four hours last month—I was afraid to tell you—she displayed all the symptoms of a curvature of the spine. It was a classical case of hysterical contraction. She imitated the curvature as if she wished to make real in her body the death of the person she loved, in order to keep him within her forever. That's too high a price to pay for repression! Besides, for me there's no longer any doubt. When she was a child, her father raped her."

"What!" She looked at me with wide eyes. "But Lucy never—"

"Because they've hidden it from her. All of them, starting with her mother. And ending up with me. And now you."

"Thank God we've at least got some tact . . ."

"Tact? If someone had raped you, do you think people could hide it from you—even if they were tactful about it?"

"I don't . . ."

"Look, in order to forget what she saw and heard, Lucy made herself blind and deaf. Now she must know—she must see, she must hear, she must live."

"But if she was a child?"

"You think as a child she didn't notice?"

"Oh, yes. But she's forgotten."

"Ha! What does that mean, to forget? It means no longer wanting to recall a memory. But where is it, that memory? Do you think it has flown away like a little bird? No! It is still inside her, unconscious, alive and throbbing in her veins. That's what repression is, that's what spoils everything. That's what provokes her anxieties, that's what disgusts her with love. By the way, did Herr O ever discuss Lucy's illness with you?"

"Yes. Once he said, 'Dr. Freud makes the unpardonable mistake of taking my daughter seriously. She thinks of herself as a martyr, but her only misfortune is that her father spoiled her too much.'"

"Nonsense. Herr O fostered her illness because it allowed him to dominate her. Hers is the *third* case of neurosis I've come across in which the patient was a victim in childhood of a sexual assault committed by an adult. Fliess agrees with me."

"Fliess?"

I gestured expansively.

"Dr. Wilhelm Fliess of Berlin. He came to Vienna last month to do some postgraduate study, met the ubiquitous Breuer, and started attending my lectures on the anatomy of the nervous system. Like me, he's highly strung, works mainly at night, suffers from migraine, and brooks very little criticism. We're each of an unsocial, taciturn disposition, unwilling to speak unless we can say something that will amaze the whole room and be handed down to posterity with all the *éclat* of a proverb. Unfortunately, at least in my case, friendships so intense and in some respects neurotic are seldom, if ever, without an undercurrent of latent hostility. People like me need to provide themselves with tyrants, I don't know why. Mine was

Breuer, for some time; then Charcot. Now, perhaps, I have found a new father-substitute to whom I can display the utmost affection, admiration, and even subservience—but somehow the latent hostility gets strengthened also."

"What does he think of *you?*"

"There's a certain mutual attraction, undeniably, though perhaps I'm the luckier one. What I relate to him from my end of the world, the psyche, finds in him an understanding critic, whereas what he tells me of his end, the stars and numbers, arouses in me only barren astonishment."

"What do you find to agree upon?"

"The centrality of sexuality, I suppose. Fliess subscribes to the sexual origin of the neuroses. 'All is sexuality,' he says, 'from volcanoes to the stars, by way of animals and men. The stars and sex—that's what produces the world and what drives it; nature is fecundity run wild.' But he insists on quantifying my 'amorphous' sexual theories, believing, for instance, that even in their smallest actions humans obey the great bisexual rhythms of the universe."

"There are so many theories of nature."

"True. And others, of course, have proved that a bisexual constitution is universal. But Fliess claims the bisexual nature of *each living cell.* He posits two entirely different kinds of sexual material, male and female, and an accompanying tendency toward periodicity in all vital activities. He speaks mystically of the tides of menstruation, the fluctuations of sexual desire; but really he talks of nothing but figures and more figures."

"I can't quite understand his attraction for you."

"Oh, I daresay there is some piece of unruly homosexual feeling at the root of the matter. No one can replace the intercourse with a friend that a particular, perhaps feminine side of me demands. I've always needed friends and enemies; it's been necessary for my equilibrium. Sometimes the friend and enemy are lodged in the same person; with Fliess, I think that's the case. And who knows? Perhaps he is right that there are instances of bisexuality in the neuroses. Perhaps there *are* two individuals in the innermost nucleus, instead of just one. I shall have to give this more thought! Meanwhile . . . I love him, I hate him. It's confused. I always find it uncanny when I can't understand someone in terms of myself!

"I'm going through a bad patch, Sophia. What's been going on inside me I really do not know. I've had to demolish some castles in Spain with Lucy, and my research is taking me Heaven knows where. In such circumstances, I thought if I could talk to someone . . . to you. Perhaps something from the deepest depths of my own neurosis is obstructing my progress in the further understanding of the neuroses, and *you* are somehow involved in it."

"What do you mean?"

"I'm not sure. I'm afraid of myself . . . of growing up, looking at the truth, letting you see what I am. Perhaps I'm afraid of loving you. I really ought to be hypnotized! Then I'd understand it better. Meanwhile the realm of the unconscious remains dark and the words of Heraclitus still stand—'The soul of man is a far country, which cannot be approached or explored.' What do you think, Sophia?"

"Of what?"

"Of a man of thirty-one who's afraid of growing up?"

She glanced at me searchingly, then averted her eyes. For a few seconds neither of us spoke. Then, slowly, and in the tone of one who has thought out a problem and come at last to a decision, she said, "You've met the Devil, Dr. Freud. He is Poseidon, Lord of the Abyss. He was waiting for you at the bottom of your own self. Let that serve as a warning to you."

I saw a piece of seaweed in blue light. "You mean . . . ?"

"I mean, perhaps, Sigmund, that things have to get worse before they can get better. The journey under the surface of the sea is always fraught with the danger of disintegration—of losing oneself in the ocean of the unknown, its vastness and formlessness. Let's hope that's it—I wish it with all my heart."

"But what's so dangerous about Poseidon?"

"As god of the creative flow, he incarnates the infinite possibilities of the fluid underworld. Water's always in movement, never the same for two successive moments . . ."

"You make him sound . . . terrible."

"He's the earth-shaker, the god of storms and tidal waves, the most primitive of the gods. His menacing nature and suppressed savagery are nonpareil. Also . . ."

"What is it?"

"I've just remembered—Poseidon's favorite fish were the thin ones on the bottom, the ones that live under such pressure they explode when they're brought to the surface."

20 June

Sunday, cloudy. Martha visiting her sister.

Knowing my interest in Atalanta, Fleischl turned up with a folio edition of Ovid's *Metamorphoses*. To my delight, it contains a description of the Calydonian boar hunt that meshes reasonably well with Lucy's version. I'll copy it here for the record (my Latin is worse than my Greek).

Ovid (43 B.C.–A.D. 18)

Now all Meleager's friends raised a glad shout,
And gathering round him, tried
To grasp his hand. The hero pressed
His conquering foot upon the boar's head
And said, "O Atalanta, glorious maid,
Of Nonacris, to you is yielded spoil.
I rejoice to share
The merit of this glorious victory."
But the envious sons of Thestius
Leveled their pointed spears and shouted out,
"Atalanta! Give up the prize!
Let not the confidence
Of your great beauty be a snare to you!"
Whereupon Meleager shouted out, "What! Ho!"
And with cruel sword pierced the breasts
Of Plexippus and Toxeus. So perished they,
And Althaea filled the city with her wild lament.
Thirsting for vengeance, she brought forth the brand
That had saved Meleager's life, and fetched a pile
Of seasoned tinder ready for the torch.
"Alas, be this the funeral pyre of my own flesh.
I am avenging and committing crime—
With death must death be justified, and crime
Be added unto crime. Let funerals
Upon succeeding funerals attend!"
She spoke, and as she turned her face away,

And threw the fatal brand on the fire,
Meleager at a distance
Felt the flame of burning wood
Scorching with secret fire his forfeit life.
With sighs and groan, he called
His aged father's name, and then the names
Of Atalanta, sisters—and last,
They say, he called upon his mother's name.
Oh! If I could tell
The grief of his unhappy sisters.
Regardless of all shame, they beat on their breasts,
Rained kisses on their loved one and his bier.
And when the flames had burnt Meleager's form,
They strained his gathered ashes to their breasts.
And Artemis, glutted with the woes
Inflicted on Porthaon's house, now gave the sisters
Some respite. She stretched long feathered wings
Upon their arms, transformed their mouths to beaks,
And sent them winging through the lucent air.

N.B. Here we are further along the road that turns myth into literature. Ovid dutifully follows the patriarchal path (Atalanta receives the boar only as a gift).

Eleven

Returning to my study after lunch, I found Fleishl's Ovid on the floor opened to a page near the back. I stooped to pick it up, intending to reshelve it, and read,

> Asking of marriage, from the Delphic god
> The maiden Atalanta drew this answer:
> "Marriage means no bliss to you;
> Yet shall it snare you, though you seek to fly;
> And you shall lose your life before you die."

Excellent discovery! The psychological ambiguity of the oracle triumphantly survives the poet's rather mannered hexameters. It's the first non-Arcadian, non-Calydonian reference I've found.

"The Delphic god" is of course Apollo.

Theocritus (c. 270 B.C.)

The oracle of Apollo at Delphi, near the foot of the south slope of Mount Parnassus, is the most famous and powerful oracle in Greece. It gives answers to all questions, public, private, religious, political, and social. The oracles are spoken by a priestess called the Pythia, who, seated on a golden tripod, utters sounds in a frenzied trance.

Plutarch (A.D. 46–120)

The Delphic oracle has been author of very great service to the Greeks in times of war and the founding of cities, on occasions of pestilence and during seasons of barrenness. Never to the present day did the language of the Pythia suffer any impeachment of its veracity.

2 July

Fliess came by to tell me he's been summoned to Berlin for an urgent consultation.

"Must you go?" I felt a sudden pain.

"You know I must. Come with me to the station."

"I . . . I don't feel very well."

"What's wrong with you?"

"An attack."

"What kind of attack?"

"Arrhythmia, feeling of suffocation, burning sensation in the region of the heart . . ."

"Nonsense—it's just a phobia. You're a man, Sigmund, a virile man; yet, as is the case with all men, a part of your makeup is feminine."

"I'm suffering from separation anxiety, that's all."

In the carriage he was silent; but at the station, walking along the platform, he suddenly said, "Let's make a pact, you the psychiatrist in Vienna, I the physiologist and mathematician in Berlin. Your patients—above all, Lucy!—provide you with the facts, I establish the periodicity of their occurrence. Rhythm, that's the key. Rhythm and number."

He took two identical gold rings out of his pocket: five-pointed stars shone on the bezels. "One for you, one for me. A secret society for two. Today there stand two men who are the only ones to know Nature's secret—sexuality drives the world. What's the matter, Sigmund? Take the ring. Are you afraid?"

I took the ring from his hand but kept it in my palm; it fell into place next to my wedding ring. There was a silence. When he spoke again it was in a harsh near-whisper. "We shall have omnipotence, Freud. We shall know all their hidden instincts, the sources of what they call Good and Evil. We shall dominate them through Reason!"

"I don't know . . ."

"Nonsense. You belong to the fraternity. A disciple of knowledge must know, mustn't he? If he doesn't *know* who he is, it's not he who's living his life; it's an Other. Find the rhythm, Freud. It will be necessary to dig deep down. Into the mud. You know that."

"What if I'm . . . not capable . . ."

"If you're not, no one will be. You must charge; it's in your character. Retreat before nothing. If your strength fails you, make a pact with the Devil. How splendid to risk Hell so that everyone can live under the light of Heaven! Meanwhile we'll write to each other every week. We'll have our own secret meetings. In ten years we shall be able to govern men. From now on we must be as close as brothers."

The train gave a jolt; he hopped aboard.

Something occurred to me. "How's your Greek, Wilhelm?"

"Not too bad, I suppose. Why?"

"Would you help me to research Delphi, the ancient oracle?"

He frowned, but I could see he would help me.

"Fine," he said, "but remember—the date of the father's birth, the date of the child's, the date of the rape."

The train started to pull out of the station.

"It's not so easy, Wilhelm." I started to run after him.

"Of course, but you'll manage. You'll perfect your method. And when I have the dates, do you know what I'll do? I'll calculate at what stage of the child's feminine or masculine period the traumatism occurred, and I can assure you that from that I'll deduce *with certainty* the nature of the illness. Take anxiety neurosis; I can tell you in a rough and ready way it's feminine. It's passivity pure and simple. Obsession is active, so it's virile. Perhaps the former appears in subjects who've been raped at the culminating moment of their feminine rhythm, the latter—"

"Will you . . . send me . . . your photograph . . .
Wilhelm?"

"Of course. Till next time, Freud!"

She refused pressure therapy. Just like that!

I am determined to try something new with her. (Rx cocaine? Can there be therapy in it, too?)

(Any reason medicinal magic shouldn't be an adjunct to
psychological therapy?)

Four minutes after the introduction of the drug she began
to converse freely and intelligently on such subjects as the
weather, her love for plants and flowers, the disposition of her
father's estates, etc. Her speech was spectacularly voluble and
free-flowing: miraculous cocaine! It's time for me to admit that
the nature of this plant is as fascinating to me as hysteria itself.
I feel a wholehearted enthusiasm for it I have felt for little else
in life. Unfortunately, for the physician to understand the nature of a drug fully, there is no other way than physiological
and pharmacological research, for which I have little inclina-
tion, and, as a neurologist in private practice, without labora-
tory connections, no proper facilities. (I should have to wait
for others to do the necessary basic research or, as an alterna-

tive, get myself appointed professor of chemistry and pharmaceutics somewhere.)

But perhaps there is another way, namely, to pioneer the relationship between physiological effect and mental effect, no special facilities needed. Perhaps others are working at it, perhaps nothing will come of it. But I believe this drug can allow me to attract the attention so essential for getting on in the world. Even if it isn't sensational, something is bound to come of it.

—⊢—

6 July

The taste was bitter and after a few minutes I was not quite myself, I seemed to be just slightly lightheaded and giddy. My eyes were watering and my throat felt full of something.

Then, over the next hour or so, the drug seemed to creep up on me and I found I could talk to Dr. F without the least difficulty. Indeed, I experienced a strange kind of mental clarity; my mind seemed to revolve and whirl like a merry-go-round, with each turn yielding the brass ring.

The euphoria was different from the intoxication of wine; I was not drunk, just happy. And thinking was not a problem; my thoughts seemed to organize themselves without conscious effort. By the time I thought of the future I had no cares in the world, no worries, no fears, no anxieties, no nerves, nothing— only bliss, a fantastic sense of well-being.

Also my apprehensions about being with a man vanished for the first time. For two hours I was as light as a feather, the queen of moving light. Dr. F and I talked about everything, time was suspended, place was boundless, the textures around me came fully alive, gripping my gaze till I could soak in their vitality. I saw an apple on a tree but refused to focus on it (since I wanted nothing, there was no need to select one item to look at rather than another)—immediately I was so flooded with the crimson of the skin that I thought I had never before known what color was.

I suppose it is a deliberate negation, a sort of active holding back from any form of action, a keeping-myself-in-leash: if I use my will to keep my attention fixed on the end I want to achieve, if I keep my muscles relaxed, my body knows how to find its own means—lines and shapes appear of themselves, I don't have to think what my limbs are doing, I can uncouple my eye from thought, let it take its own course, since it has quite definite interests of its own, as shapes and lines have movements of their own. I can spread wide my invisible feelers of mind, push myself out into the landscape, into the movements of air—

Afterward I was struck by one amazing fact, that I had not once thought of H.

⸻

9 July

Sitting in her chair like a strange oak queen, almost supernatural in her glowing smiling richness, Sophia gave me tea in her studio. After some chitchat I asked her, "Can you tell me anything about Delphi?"

"Sigmund! How strange that you should mention Delphi."

"Why?"

"Perhaps every approach to the oracle is prophetic. It's the site of our next dig, you see. Before he got sick, Heinrich took a house on Parnassus to work on his next book—on Calydon."

"You mean . . . Delphi's close to Calydon?"

"Just up the hill."

"So is that a reason for locating Atalanta at Delphi?"

"Why not? Her placement at Delphi would speak eloquently of the transition there from open-air worship associated with a sacred tree or stone to worship in a temple, with the god conceived of as anthropomorphic in shape."

"The god being Apollo."

"Yes—the ultimate European male, the blond Hellenic ideal of masculine grace and dignity, the god more Olympian than any other, more radiantly splendid, more aloof, more utterly in the fullest sense of the word 'superior.' Apollo represents the victorious splendor of clarity, the intelligent sway of order and moderation. He's the peculiar god, the tribal god, of the Dorians; but he seems to have been originally a Hellenic god, common to all the Hellenic tribes. Reason, nobility, form, action, apprehension—the list of his attributes is endless. He's the god of prophecy, of medicine, of light in art as well as nature."

"Did you say medicine?"

She smiled. "Apollo is your patron saint, Sigmund, the god of scientific truth. He cannot deceive and cannot himself be deceived—the very opposite of mantic, self-deceiving Poseidon."

"I'm not sure I'm being complimented."

"You're Apollo come to life: 'Let's shed light fully and

everywhere, even if it means violating people's souls in order to cure them by means of the truth.' "

I was annoyed. "Why not? When dawn's approaching, I'm willing to help the day break through."

"But you're missing half of time, half of life. Look at Apollonian temple-worship."

"Well?"

"In ancient times, as if to dramatize the contrast between the god's clarity and balance and the irrational, awesome power of raw nature, the abstract mathematical order of the temples was always set against the primordial wildness of the earth. Nowhere was this truer than at Delphi, a site peculiarly prone to earthquakes. Of course, it's not easy to unweave the tissue of half-truths and legends the Greeks have woven around their central shrine; but the order of the different movements, as given by mythographers, is substantially the same. Older, darker cults existed at Delphi before the northerners planted the Apollonian worship at the foot of snow-crowned Parnassus. The original possessor of the oracle was Earth, the Universal Mother, known variously as Our Lady of the Wild Things, the Triple Goddess, Isis, the Great Mother, Artemis, Ishtar, Gaia, and the Minoan Mistress of Beasts.

"Now listen to this. According to Homer, Apollo was Artemis' twin brother, the *younger* twin—so it's just not tenable that at Delphi, where Apollo reigned supreme, his older sister should be so strangely, significantly absent. Artemis as Mother *must* have been present, along with a subordinate male consort; then, when patriarchy ousted matriarchy, the two were recast in the barren relation of sister and brother. Finally, the female figure dwindled altogether and the male consort emerged as utterer of Zeus' will."

"And perpetuated the oracle? Why?"

"Perhaps he had to—perhaps that's how the Pythia was forced on him. Euripides says that 'Earth, to avenge herself, sent up dreams which revealed unto the cities of mortals the past and the future.'"

"Wait a minute. Who was the Pythia?"

"The priestess of Apollo. In early times she was appointed as a young virgin; then, at some uncertain date when one of them was seduced by a suppliant, the Delphic authorities decided to employ only women over—"

I interrupted. "I wonder if the woman chosen was of a specially susceptible temperament, such as a neurotic or hysterical subject."

"Plutarch only says 'the Pythia should be a free-born Delphian who has acquired nothing from art or training or help of any sort. Before ascending the god's holy tripod, the three-legged stool consecrated in the innermost sanctuary, she has her soul free from perturbation; afterward, when she has departed from the tripod and the inspiration is past, she continues in calm and peace.'"

"You know these words—"

"I learned them from my husband. The moment of congress with Apollo, when the Pythia mounts the tripod over the chasm, inhales the divine afflatus, and bursts forth into wild prophetic utterance—this moment was the cornerstone of the ancient world. Unfortunately, we do not possess a single straightforward account telling in prose what the procedure at Delphi was. We know the direct prophecies of the Pythia were uttered on only one day in each month—'shortly after dawn on the seventh.' At other times other procedures were available, such as augury derived from the flight or cry of birds, called primordial revelation; divination by fire; the examination of entrails; the interpretation of omens, and so on. The oldest method of divination at Delphi was oneiromancy, or divination by dreams, particularly under the form of incubation, as it was called."

"What precisely was incubation?"

"Who knows? Artemis was the goddess of man's life as one with nature, a communion, not a segregation; Apollo is the god of man's articulate life, separate from the rest of nature, a purely human accomplishment. What's been lost in transition is the eternal healing of dispassionate nature as against the angry clash of irreconcilable human wills and egotisms. It's difficult to realize now how important it was to the ancient world, this shift of attention, of religious focus, from Earth to Sky, from Mother to Apollo, from a gaze that was on the coming and going of the fruits of the earth and the disorderly and fearful phenomena of the weather to a contemplation of the fixed and orderly procession of the heavenly bodies. When Apollo ousted his sister from Delphi, it was the sacrifice of Earth to Logic—of the whole gynecocratic order of the Minoan-Mycenaean world to the ordering, classifying, mastering reason of the Dorians, with their mania for petty arithmetic. Civilization had advanced; the old intense interest in food and the recurrent fertility of the earth had slackened. People tend, in their search for food, to focus their attention first on the ground and only later on the sky. The calendar is at first seasonal, based not on observation of the heavenly bodies but on the waxing and waning of plants. Only afterward is it noticed that life depends on moisture—that heaven and the weather, rain, wind, and storm, influence the food supply."

"Is it possible to ask you a psychological question? What about Apollo's sexuality?"

"Love was the area in which the god of reason was least at home. The myths of his adventures with women are dominated by unsuccessful chases and fleeing maidens. This god who wonderfully embodies light and truth and masculine beauty wreaks destruction in the world of love and the feminine. Apollonian willpower is a very insignificant force to pit against Aphrodite. She represents life. To resist her is as futile as resisting life. And those who imagine themselves immune to her power are the very ones on whom her wrath descends most vigorously—her myths are full of vengefulness against those who forget her."

"Like those of Artemis . . . My head is spinning."

"You must learn to be more human. Your coldness is forbidding, Sigmund. Why do you bury your feelings toward me under a hierarchical submission to my husband?" Her eyes, as they bored into mine, seemed suddenly to know everything about me, to believe in me, wish me well, trust me to go on with my work. "The survival of the Triple Goddess always depends on men's remembering that whole of life of which they are a specialized fragment. Some very great scientists have attested to the fact that there is nothing exclusively rational and objective about science. Intuition, inspiration, enthusiasm—all the gifts of the Mother—are at least as important in scientific discovery as Apollonian logic, discipline, and clarity. But the development of the Artemisian attitude beyond the purely physiological has never been intellectually understood—although a feminine stance is really just as legitimate, intellectually and biologically, as a masculine one. Don't you agree, my handsome golden Apollo?"

16 July

Night. Never have I experienced such agony. More than anything I would like to describe successfully her face, her ways; but I cannot, because my desire for her blinds me when I think of her.

(How will I ever break her spell? By incarnating her in another? Isn't this the talent of the Mother?)

17 July

Instead of administering the drug I decided to talk to her about sex in the general way of physicians and young girls. "You know, Lucy, with the female sex, the physician's complaint about the underestimation of the sexual factor is justified. With girls who suffer from hysteria we never mention masturbation, while in the case of young men we immediately look for pollutions."

Silence. Neither did she look at me.

I continued. "I would say in this respect we physicians are actually in a state of hysteria; we repress a feeling that is unpleasant to us. We know nothing about the sexuality of girls and women—no physician has any idea what sorts of symptoms an erection evokes in women, because the young ones do not want to talk about it and the old ones have already forgotten—but we ask nothing."

No response. I felt only a void when I looked at her.

Letter from Fliess
17 July

Dear Sigmund,

In classical times the oracular cave at Delphi was essentially a place of counsel for practical purposes, a place to be consulted for advice as to the immediate future. The innermost sanctuary contained various laurel branches and votive ribbons, the tomb of Poseidon, a golden statue of Apollo, his lyre and sacred armor, his golden tripod (three metal legs supporting a bowl for offerings or incense), his jawbone, his genitals, his navel string, and finally the famous *omphalos*.

The *omphalos* was the oldest object of cult preserved at Delphi, an egg-shaped stone that marked the navel (*omphalos*), or center, of the Earth. Dating back to the times before religious belief became articulate, it was mounted on a rectangular base, the hole in the base fitting the hole in the omphalos.

Before the second or third millenium B.C., the *omphalos* was just a fetish worshipped or feared for its own inner power; then, when Greek religion assumed a more personal form, Delphi became the cosmic spinal cord, the vertical geometry that locked the soul into eternity—and the base of the whole thing was the *omphalos*, the base of the cosmic axis. It was believed that heavenly bodies and pilgrims on earth were connected to one another, alike in orbital motion, cycling, ascending, and descending through a slowly turning, everywhere interjoined cosmic system. Of course, access to the star-fields could be had at any site where the sea flowed plainly into the sky at the horizon, but Parnassus was special—the star-mountain, the World Mountain over which the Pole Star shone. Fixed between zenith and nadir, oriented to the four directions, it was the axis that separated and joined, the place where separate worlds had their point of intersection and annihilated the one that was of rivers and trees.

For the pilgrim, the approach to Delphi took place on the wheel of the ecliptic, around the sun, alongside the moon and planets, and against a background of precessing stars. Carrying the image of the *omphalos* in his brain cells, the pilgrim traveled around his own center, his own temple; and as he turned through the axis of his thought, he was just one more particle in a work of the imagination that was both illusion and reality.

Spectacularly prone to earthquakes, Delphi was nonetheless home to a famous pre-Hellenic statue of Psyche (it was kept in a bin of sand). Now, this couldn't have been the beautiful, moody, suicidal girl of myth who settles down with Eros, the one we laughed about at school. *Her* wanderings, including her descent to the lower world, first occur in Apuleius' Latin novel *The Golden Ass,* written in the second century A.D. As for the word "psyche" itself, it's grammatically feminine in Greek (ψυχή) and originally meant breath, then life, then the animating principle in man and other living beings, the source of vital activities rational or irrational. It's the oldest, most primitive hypothesis adopted by the Greeks to explain the phenomena of dreams, swoons, and ecstatic visions.

One last thing. During the seventh and eighth centuries A.D., a Buddhist cult emerged at Delphi which combined Tibetan with earlier Pelasgian geocosmological ideas. This syncretic cult taught the existence of a Golden Point in space, where two realms of being and nonbeing collide, a point that occurs at the beginning of a given world cycle but is recoverable (in other words, it is repeatable). Do you suppose our ancestors had already agreed to humanity's progressive decadence—biologically, ethically, spiritually—and knew their only hope was the "return," the periodic resumption by all beings of their former lives?

Is this the kind of thing you wanted?

Have you been keeping to four cigars?

18 July

I feel I'm on the verge of uncovering a secret of nature, a lightning bolt that will fuse biology and psychology and prove the distinction, or lack of it, between mind and body, physical and emotional states.

Let me adduce my evidence. First, the geographical evidence—

The earliest authorities agree that a physical cause unique to Delphi and Parnassus (possibly some mephitic gas ascending from a fissure in the earth) cooperated, or was even the leading agency, in the Pythian frenzy. There are hints from the Stoics of inspiration produced by *pneuma*, a breath regarded as something midway between material and nonmaterial, a breath capable of providing a sun-flare of creative activity. In later times, of course, a wholly material cause of prophetic intoxication was posited, namely laurel, the sacred tree of Apollo (after he captured it from the earth-goddess). In Plutarch there's evidence that the chewing of laurel leaves was supposed to bring the seeker into touch with the gods; it was routinely used by prophets and poets to invoke inspiration.

Second, the mythological-astronomical evidence—

Sometime during the first Olympiad, when the men's games were assimilated as closely as possible with the women's, the laurel leaf was substituted—on the authority of the Delphic oracle—for the original apple bough as the prize of victory. It must have worked as follows: the lunar calendar was superseded by the agricultural calendar, then combined with, then superseded by, faster (daily) solar time.

Third, the botanical evidence—

A system that has absorbed even an extremely small amount of cocaine is capable of amassing (purely as a result of the reaction of the body to coca) a greater store of vital energy, which can be converted into work, than would have been possible without coca. In other words, if we take the amount of work as being constant, the body that has absorbed cocaine is able to manage with a lower metabolism, which in turn means a smaller intake of food. It might be objected that labor that draws upon food or tissue components *always* involves a certain loss, either in the utilization of assimilated food or in the conversion of energy into work, but surely this loss could be drastically reduced if appropriate steps were taken—for example, a stronger dose of the drug to effect the optimum availability of materials already stored in the body, even perhaps to obviate eventual replacement of those materials. By exciting the nerve centers, such a drug, whatever its name or provenance, could nourish the body completely without food!

I feel I am panning for scientific gold! Why not? Science is always a race. If it is already possible to stain nervous tissue with a solution of gold chloride, and the metal's effect on the nerve endings gives a wonderfully clear and precise picture of the cells and fibers . . .

What if the nervous system itself, the wiring, the diagram underlying pain perception—what if it could be treated directly by a drug? What would such a drug be worth? What price could one pay for the creative force of psychological metamorphosis submerged in the human nervous system?

It makes sense, but seems too fantastic.

Such a golden fruit, if it existed, would have to walk the line between food and drug. The toxin would have to exist in just the proper concentration to produce the right effect . . .

Could a golden tree like that emerge from the depths of prehistory with its fruit still shaking? Could it be possible because plants and animals share structurally similar chemicals even after a million years of evolution? Could the earth, with all its minerals and plants and creatures, be so very simple and unified?

I've just thought: the Trojan War supposedly began with Paris awarding the Apple of Discord to Aphrodite ("for the fairest"). But it's backwards! It's as clear as day to me that the ancient icon of the Three Goddesses, the one that has been iconotropically interpreted as Paris adjudicating the apple to Aphrodite, has an entirely different meaning. To award an apple to the love-goddess would be an impertinence on Paris' part; all apples were hers. No; obviously the three goddesses are, as usual, the three members of the ancient Triple Goddess. Aphrodite is *giving* the apple to Paris, not receiving it from him. Adam was created from Eve, not the other way round; she is, in fact, his mother!

Twelve

5 Maria Theresienstrasse

24 July

Last night, with Martha, I was performing vacuous motions, and I realized for the first time that I didn't have any idea why I was doing it. I seem to have lost completely my youthful ambition to prove my physical and sexual prowess! The activity to which Martha and I are presently devoting ourselves seems to have more of a symbolic character than a physical one.

What are these motions we are performing supposed to symbolize? Tenderness? Love? Health? *Joi de vivre?*

Friendship? A plea for long life?

"You're not wearing your ring."

"Wilhelm! When did you get back?"

"I arrived this morning for a week or two."

"Come in! What luck! You're the only person who can help me. The maddest things are occurring to me; I'm over-stimulated and depressed at the same time. There are spells where consciousness is greatly narrowed, states difficult to describe, with a veil that produces almost a twilight condition of mind. Last Friday, after cutting back to four cigars as per your suggestion, there suddenly came a severe affliction of the heart, worse than I ever had when smoking fifteen cigars—"

"Cardiac symptoms?"

"The maddest racing and irregularity, constant tension, oppression, hot pain down the left arm, some dyspnea of a suspiciously organic degree . . . and with it all, Wilhelm, an oppression of mood in which images of dying and farewell predominate with strange theories."

"Strange theories?"

"There are days when everything sickens me and I think how sweet it must be to die. I am in a cocoon and God knows what kind of beast will creep out of it."

He took on a stubborn look. "I'm not a psychiatrist, you know, Freud."

"Wilhelm, I want you to hypnotize me."

"No, I don't know how to. Anyway, you're not neurotic. We're a team, Freud. You've got no right to have these problems of conscience. At Breuer's you offered me something solid—a method, hypnotic investigation; a result, sexual traumatism. But now I no longer follow you."

"But I want . . ."

"Why on earth do you need to analyze your every state of mind? The things you say! From anyone else I would call them scientific fairy tales."

"But Wilhelm . . . I'm not evil, am I?"

"Come on, now, you know very well you're not."

"Well, whatever possessed me to discover universal vileness? I can't stand looking into the void any longer. If my sexual theory's true, men really are swine."

"Why not? The only question is to establish it scientifically. We know that hatred is masculine, love feminine—"

I started to laugh. Fliess hissed, "You are too much of a preacher, Freud. You are really a priest. You can't hear what anybody else has to say, your own voice is so loud. It makes talking to you impossible. Why won't you allow that there is any mind other than your own? Why do you seem to have a lurking desire to have your gizzard slit and imagine every man has his knife up his sleeve for you?"

"How do you make that out?"

"From you."

There was a pause of enmity between us, near to hate and near to love. It is always the same with us. Always our talk brings us into a deadly nearness of contact, a strange, perilous intimacy that is either hate or love or both. We part with apparent unconcern, as if our going apart were a trivial occurrence, yet though we agree to keep it to the level of trivial occurrence, we burn with each other inwardly.

"Look, my friend," he said now. "I need your theory of traumatisms for my calculations. I grant you may have made errors of detail. Very well, find them. Correct them. But don't dig down into yourself anymore. You'll go mad if you try to know yourself. We're not made for that. Where does science come into all that? It's nothing but cock-and-bull stories. I can't build anything on it. Thinking means measuring. Have you taken any measurements? Established any quantitative ratios?"

"No."

"Then it's all quackery!"

"Take care, Fliess. You talk of nothing but figures and measurements, but when it comes down to it I wonder whether you don't tailor your calculations to produce whatever final results you've been aiming at from the outset."

He smiled so hugely, so winningly, that I could not keep from smiling myself. And so for five or ten seconds we smiled frankly and affectionately at each other, and our souls nodded to each other through the windows of our eyes like neighbors who have never really greeted each other but now lean out of their windows at the same moment. My admiration for him grew, along with the suspicion that he was trying to blind me and dupe me and lead me into a trap with his enigmatic, conceited generalizations.

"A man should do what his demon drives him to do, Freud; but you seem to have the simultaneous air of a soul in torment and a conqueror. Tell me, what is there in your psychology besides unscientific bravado? What other elements are there except pure romanticism? It's romantic from every point of view."

I said with sudden decision, "Wilhelm, I want to introduce you to Sophia Schliemann. Let's all go climbing together this weekend."

"Why?"

"There's a dreamlike quality about her. She seems to cast a radiance wherever she goes."

"You're in love with her?"

"Possibly. She seems to be changing my relation to Martha."

"Beware of ascribing to her that which is essentially your own."

"Meaning?"

"There are two sorts of women—the woman-trinket that one can handle and manipulate, who is an ornament in a man's life, and the woman-landscape that one visits, enters into, may get lost in. The first is vertical, voluble, capricious, demanding, a coquette. The other is horizontal, taciturn, obstinate, possessive, dreamy, and has a long memory."

"And you prefer?"

"Me? I'm convinced that I could live my life as a monk in spite of the brutal voluptuousness with which I am gifted, and which I always call forth. I am always master of myself when I want to be."

28 July

Sunday excursion to the mountain in the Semmering neighborhood (not exactly an alp, but more challenging than anything in the Prater). Sophia wore a light Tyrolean leather jacket and plumed hat; Wilhelm and I had not traded trousers for shorts but wore mountain shoes and carried alpenstocks.

By midmorning we had reached a height of about three thousand feet. Above us were high mountain pastures and snowy peaks, around us bare rock and scree, below that the valley. Sophia gave off a flame of eagerness that caught Wilhelm as well as me; her gaze seemed pantheistically daring, rash in expectancy. The air seemed to ring with her. She seemed to be saying, "Are you prepared to view the extraordinary?"

I said to her, "Don't you adore seeing things from on high, Sophia?"

"Nearer to God, Sigmund? Or further away from people?"

"The higher I go, the better it suits me."

"If I were a certain Dr. Freud, I'd draw the conclusion that you like to dominate."

"Shall we begin our descent?" Fliess asked. Gesturing to a path overrun with boulders, he suggested that we scramble down through the scree to rejoin the main path some two hundred yards below.

I agreed and went down first. Sophia followed like a practiced climber, going down sideways across the scree. Then Wilhelm went down facing forward, with the result that he slipped and fell on his back, cursing. Sophia climbed back up to help him, but he regained his feet unaided, brushed his trousers, and managed to laugh at his misadventure.

"Thank heaven I don't invest my pride in mountain climbing."

"You slipped because you fastened your eyes on the peaks rather than the valley, Dr. Fliess. Do the same as me—go down sideways. You're quite safe, and you can brake."

She started down again. Fliess, imitating her this time,

followed quite a way behind. When he reached the bottom, he lighted a cigar. I was surprised; usually he smokes only after meals.

"If you're going to smoke," said Sophia, "let us at least sit down."

We left the path and sat on a flat rock, all of us staring at the waterless bed of a stream that meandered between some trees.

"What is your theory of hysteria, Dr. Fliess?" she asked.

"I?" There was a peculiar glint in his eyes, as if he were trapped between pleasure and exposure. "Well, as you know, the name announces that the illness is feminine; 'hysteria' comes from the Greek word for uterus. The sole prescription for such a malady is familiar enough to us, but we cannot order it. It runs *Rx Penis normalis; dosim repetatur.*"

"Really, Fliess," I objected. "The uterine theory of hysteria is hopelessly out of date, you know that. It's much too teleologically oriented to say 'The uterus has an ardent desire to create children' or 'The uterus becomes unhappy and angry if the womb remains empty for too long after its owner's puberty.' "

"What! Can this be you, Freud, a materialist and an atheist, denying Aristotle and giving in to womanish superstitions?"

"Since I'm an atheist I have to be superstitious; otherwise, what would be left?"

"*Touché!*" said Sophia. "Even you, Dr. Fliess, have to admit that here on this earth we are hemmed in by mystery—in our homes, in the street, everywhere when we come to think of it."

"I agree with her, Wilhelm. Isn't it really the part of shallowness to account for *everything* by attributing it to the movement of molecules? Doesn't a chance encounter often decide the entire life of a man?"

His beard, in the direct sunlight, gave off a strange metallic blue reflection. The jet-black hair seemed to have concentric circles of darker black or blue in it, producing the effect of watered silk. "Don't examine yourself too closely, Freud," he said, pouring water over everyone. "The time for fantasies is past—we're not twenty-year-old boys any longer." He was certainly in a most peculiar mood, reflective yet excited. "Besides, it's never comfortable on the summits. An icy wind blows and everyone crouches, watchful lest his neighbor hurl him down the precipice. There can be only one sun; such is the order of nature, and anything else is a heresy."

"Where do so much stubbornness, aggression, and hatred come from, Dr. Fliess?" Sophia's beautiful face had grown pale to the very lips, and there was a blackness about her eyes. "You are the ultimate flower of rational astigmatism, a man who gets his instincts from below and his thoughts from on high. You crush the feminine impulses, you relegate them to the darkness. Then, if they should lift their heads, you gag them and kill them. That makes real men, you think—adults, worthy of the freedom they've won. The iron heel! The iron heel on the loins of the beast!"

"Medicine is action—" Fliess began.

She cut him off: "You do not act, Dr. Fliess, but merely work; and so you miss the darkest mysteries, the most vibrant meanings. Oh, I believe there are no longer any human beings, only occupations!" She rose and walked some way away. I followed her, and Fliess brought up the rear, exhaling a cloud of black smoke. By mutual consent we walked the mile or so to the Semmering dancing hall *cum* restaurant and sat at a table. A bottle of champagne was brought. We sat stiffly and dumbly in our chairs, drank to each other in silence, regarded the hall and its decorations, and stared at the dancers who were revolving in the middle of the floor.

Fliess' face took on a hard expression, and the lines at the sides of his mouth deepened. "You know, Mrs. Schliemann, now and then in this world I have come across people whose talk and companionship have given me pleasure. But I do not count in the least on your affection or on anyone else's. Life-long friendships happen at eighteen. At thirty one has done with that sort of thing; all one's devotion is required for self. For the most part I have ceased to care for people and can part from them without regret. My emotions have seen too much service, I have made too many calls upon them for them not to show signs of wear and tear. I can describe them as sentiments reserved for special occasions."

"For instance, what occasions?"

"For special occasions. I am taking steps to secure my health of mind. The cure consists of ceasing to rack my brains on certain subjects and putting a curb on my emotions. Time and dissipation are the two sovereign remedies. In the end the heart grows callous, and then one ceases to suffer. You may say such conduct reveals appalling depths of selfishness; I do not deny it. But I have come to the conclusion that I have a right to do as I please—that this insipid banquet of life requires all the spice that one can lend it. I, Cain, go alone as I deserve; but my punishment is not greater than I can bear."

He fell silent, as powerful as stone in the force of his silence, with an innate, elementary grandeur. With his mouth firmly set, the squareness of his jaw being unduly marked, he said, "Wait till you cool down, Mrs. Schliemann. You will see things the same way as I do."

"You may be the one to cool first." She faced him. "What will you become, Dr. Fliess? What will keep you in this world? What will impel you from patient to patient?" She made a vague gesture, as if urging him to greater discretion. "You are not a genius, but you may be one of those people with a gifted normal intellect who moves upward to icy, abnormal spheres of comprehension and moral isolation, to a frightful, criminal degree of knowingness. Just make sure you die not one moment before you are released from the desire to live."

We left the dancing hall; twilight was seeping steadily into the sky, coloring it a greenish-grayish blue. There was a subtle feeling in the air, something infiltrating one's mood and making it tender and a little melancholy, susceptible to all kinds of delicate and barely perceptible agitations.

I am not sure what to think about Fliess. I suppose he has reached the point at which great men must leave the path of tradition and, trusting to supreme, indefinable powers, strike out on new, trackless courses where experience is no guide. He seems to suffer a Promethean, a Luciferian, isolation—that of the too greatly daring, the damned.

As for Sophia, I have given up analyzing her. Perhaps she is a woman who can only be understood by a man who dreams of being a woman himself.

3 August

After the session I was walking down toward the gate to intercept the carriage that would take me home when I heard a low rippling laugh above my head and caught sight of Lucy running along a tree branch over my head. I stopped in my tracks, my heart pounding with terror. Lucy! She was at least thirty feet above the ground. Her face in the sky was as deep blue as a sapphire, strangely distinct, as if it emitted a radiance of its own. A stream of energy passed between us. For a minute or more I stood transfixed, gazing upward as if I were engaged in the open-eyed adoration of a holy person or image.

Suddenly she disappeared; then just as suddenly, two or three minutes later, she materialized at my side, barefooted. Though I had seen her indoors twenty minutes before, I gaped at her. The improvement in her general condition is obvious in natural light. The waxen tinge has left her skin and a warm rose-gold shows right through it. Her hair has grown thicker and healthier looking, and she's got a bright color. Apparently the drug agrees with her.

With a smile she sat down on the grass, cool green skirt ballooning next to me, and I sat down as well. In her lap she held a ripe golden pear, which she threw into the air, catching it with a cupped, polished palm. It occurred to me, what would I not give to kiss her delicate-boned long-fingered bird-like hand (the one with the fruit)? Accordingly I took her hand in mine and held and stroked and squeezed it. She glanced at me with an expression at once provocative and fearful. I heard a pure ringing sound in my ears and felt a rush of roaring black time. A thought passed through my mind that I was demented and was about to do something stupid.

"Talk to me," I said to her desperately.

"What about?"

"Anything that comes into your mind."

"My mind's completely empty." She threw back her head and her teeth rested for a while on her glistening under-lip.

I took the fruit from her hand and bit into it.

"Give it back," she said.

"No."

I wrestled with her for the fruit, bit into it again, started to chew. She pretended to be furious but brought her head down close to my chewing mouth. When her hair touched my temple and her arm brushed my cheek I pressed my lips to her wrist. Then I put my arms around her. She twisted herself free and lay back on her elbows. With perfect simplicity, she extended her legs across my lap.

My pulse was 40 one second, 100 the next.

Her legs twitched. I stroked them. Subtly I shifted my weight several times until every movement we made, every shuffle and ripple, improved the tactile correspondence between us. Under my glancing fingertips, the minute hairs along her shins started bristling ever so slightly as she yielded to the pressure of my hands and stretched out her legs wider. There was a yellowish violet bruise on her inner thigh, which my hand massaged and slowly enveloped; then, because of her rather perfunctory underthings, there seemed to be nothing to prevent my thumb from reaching the hollow, just as you might tickle and caress a giggling child. A dreamy, eerie expression, half pleasure, half pain, came over her features. I was afraid I might go too far and cause her to start back in revulsion and terror; but luckily, years of secret sufferings have taught me superhuman self-control.

Thirteen

5 Maria Theresienstrasse

4 August

Spent the morning musing, pacing, reading, fully digesting my almost-experience of yesterday. I'm proud that I have stolen a pleasant spasm without impairing the doctor-patient relationship. Absolutely no harm has been done. Lucy is safe and I am safe with her. (What I had finally touched was not Lucy at all but my own creation, a fanciful Lucy, more real than Lucy, overlapping and encasing her, floating between me and her but having no will, no consciousness, no life of its own. The actual child knows nothing. I have done nothing to her. And nothing would induce me to repeat a performance that seems to have affected her so little.)

I'm afraid of losing Martha. She knows nothing but she guesses.

I said to her at breakfast, "I want to talk to you about Lucy."

"Don't let's talk about her."

"But we must talk about her!"

"Why? I know what you're going to say—that you don't feel any love for her, not even any desire; that you haven't been trying to seduce her; that her feelings for you are a byproduct of the treatment; that you'll always be faithful to me. What's the use? I'm quite convinced of all that."

"Well, then?"

"I don't like it—the new hypnosis, whatever it is. Do you really believe it's a scientific method of treatment? I find it unsavory."

"Martha . . ."

"In the old days you used to tell me things. Now you keep silent, but the look in your eyes frightens me."

"Don't be jealous."

"It's not jealousy, Sigmund, it's disgust. Reflect carefully. Are you sure a woman can live with a husband whose occupation disgusts her? Won't you give up this therapy with her?"

I looked at her with a kind of despairing passion. "You know very well it's impossible to go backward."

"Even if you're in danger of destroying yourself? Even for the sake of our happiness?"

"Not even for the sake of our happiness, Martha. Science is inhuman. Besides, it's not me. It's somebody else. Somebody who resembles me, perhaps . . . whom she loves without admitting it to herself. She loves me—if she does—instead of that man."

"What man?"

"I don't know. In some ways her father's still alive. It's a displacement of her feelings. I'm just an image of the other, a symbol. She has made a transference onto me."

" 'Transference.' What a fine word!" She blinked her eyes. "My love for you, was that a transference?"

"Why not?"

"Then we only ever love shadows?"

"I don't know, Martha. It's something I've just understood. I'll see where it leads me. Maybe transference is the normal relationship between the doctor and the neurotic patient."

"It's dirty, the way you exploit it."

"How about an illness, do you think that is clean? All doctors must take risks."

"But they know where they're going and you don't. You'll trick your patients, you'll force them. You must give it up!"

"Give what up?"

"Stop, if there's still time!"

"Martha! What would become of science if men of learning did not say what they believe to be the truth? I cannot conceive of a healthy society that's built on lies!"

"Society? What's that? Oh, yes. Of course, I remember. Wasn't it yesterday? Yesterday, but a century ago. In this city, but on a planet that is now far away. How everything gets confused—times, places, the world broken in pieces, not to be glued back together again. Only the memory—that's the only remnant of life."

5 August

Not really daring to let myself go, not actually kissing her, I touched the opening lips with the utmost piety, tiny sips, nothing more; but then she bent her head with a soft slow languid movement and her breath came near to my face and my arms went under her knees and I was stumbling downward with her toward the river. With her eyes closed, her grave pure face seemed to mask no mind at all; yet it wasn't inane, it wasn't null, it was full and alive with itself, perhaps rather innocent but fascinating, as fascinating as the slim magnificent body and limbs with their splendidly muscular contours and pure but opulent color.

I stopped near the river, placed her on the grass, and appraised her inch by inch, the lithe suntanned feet and legs, the fine rich shoulders, the perfect flat cushions of the undeveloped white breasts. She opened her eyes deliberately, large long eyes, childishly sweet yet wonderfully strong and wistful in expression, the irises a greenish brown with amber sparks in them. Her forehead twitched and her eyes fixed their regard, like a cat's, upon me.

"I don't understand," she said.

"But you will obey?"

"I will obey."

The sun streamed and pulsated in the surrounding trees. I thought, I am the cleverest, tenderest, unhappiest, most dreadful of all men. I knelt and, fumbling with my clothes, gave her to hold in her hand the scepter of my passion. She twitched her fingers as she felt it. I watched her face, beyond the veil of my delight, unaware of it, alien to it—then I entered her and passed into that plane of being where nothing matters except the infusion of joy brewed within the body. Slowly what had begun as a delicious distension of my innermost roots became a glowing tingle that reached that state of absolute security, confidence, and reliance not found elsewhere in conscious life. The nerves of pleasure were all laid bare. I was above the tribulations of ridicule, beyond the possibilities of retribution. The least pressure would suffice to set paradise loose.

Afterward she had the perfect candor of creation. She was so new and frail, like a flower made perfect by inner light, so wonderfully undimmed that I could not bear to look at her. She seemed no longer a being apart but a sacred part of me; and this knowledge seemed to mix with her flesh, to purify and exalt it, to make it infinitely sweet and precious. We had come together, she the moon and I the sun, two halves of one whole. Her soul was so new, so undefined, so glimmering with the unseen; and my soul was dark and gloomy, it had only one grain of living hope, like a grain of mustard seed.

She rolled away from me and got up onto her knees, smiling as if ashamed with a soft still smile, her face flushing with confusion and shame. She stood up. With each second that passed her confusion took an increasing hold on her. After perhaps a minute she began shaking her fist, threatening me from where she stood. At first her gesture seemed ridiculous— the tiny fist, the shakes—but I went over to her and kissed her on the forehead. Mingled with my guilt was the thought that her mood might prevent me from making love to her again. When she fainted I bent over her, lifted her eyelids, and looked at the whites: smarting pink like an opal dissolving within a pool, a last dab of color, stinging red . . .

At home I lay on my back and stared at the ceiling. I was exhausted, but sleep took forever to come.

Why am I so vulnerable? Why am I unable to understand or resist?

I am a bomb, ticking. I blame the drug. It could destroy everything.

—⊢—

5 August

I smell the smell of the encircling forest. I fly into the shadow of a gully, across it through glistening space, space that hangs suspended so that little sounds wander here and there, lose themselves, and are drowned. I see the flickering leaf-shadows, blue or green, I don't know which, but I feel them in my bones. A splash of sunlight leaps against the darkness, the gold flows richly in my eyes, flows through my brain in still pools of light.

Sounds: the air is full of sounds and sighs, the sighs of wind in the trees, sighs that fade back into the overhanging silence. A bee passes, a golden ripple in the air; underneath, a chicken fussily crunches a blade of grass . . .

That pine—my eye is led up and down the straightness of its trunk, my muscles feel its roots spreading wide to hold it upright against the hill. I sit motionless on its branch, draining sensation to the depths, wave after wave of delight flowing through my body. I feel clear, transparent, all parts of me smooth, cool-eyed. I sink all the way down and let the tide of my real being take me—flickering here and there like a butterfly, effortless, following my pleasure, resting on various thoughts that no longer make a barrier between me and what I see but are woven into the texture of my seeing . . .

The chirp of passing sparrows becomes the center of a thought; it makes its visual pattern against the murmuring dark emptiness of space, a never-ending murmuring sea of space above my head, beneath my feet, on every side . . .

The ground streams away under my feet; everything goes rippling out in circle upon circle; I swoop down into the hollows; the blurred landscape far ahead divides and makes an aisle for me, bursts into leaf as I pass; I slip through village after village, taking everything in at a glance as though I were some vast bird wheeling at a great height, taking my bird's-eye view of the revolving world . . .

Now there are dark spots in the air . . . spots like islands . . . seldom visited. Now they're clustering thicker than before . . . lying at the approach to a peninsula fallen into the sea . . .

<hr />

6 August

Lucy and Sophia have disappeared! The servants have been bribed! I have lost her!

Martha knows, Breuer; Wilhelm?

A dream:

Entering a cave, I see, opposite me, at the far end of the cave, my mother, Amalia Freud, dressed like a Byzantine empress, her bare arms, neck, and shoulders covered with numerous jewels. She sits on a throne carved from solid rock.

I smile and wave my hand. There is a living snake coiled round her waist. She remains impassive, reticent, her arms folded in her lap. I approach and caress her arms and shoulders in a very sensual manner. Neither of us speaks. She looks at me with a vaguely mocking expression. I am about to kiss her, when I wake up.

The Lost
Dream

Fourteen

5 Maria Theresienstrasse
3 April 1888

I am reopening the case. (It's as if a marvelous, heaven-scented flower, buzzing with golden bees, had suddenly sprung up inside me.) This morning I received a short note from Sophia Schliemann: "Lucy is with me, at my dig in Delphi. She wishes to consult a physician. Please come."

I showed the note to Martha, and admitted I had hypnotized Lucy against seeing other physicians, as a precaution. What a relief to tell someone! (Personal intimacy would not have been a sufficient reason; it also took our intellectual honesty with each other.)

I have purchased rail tickets through to Venice and will proceed by sea to Itea in Phocis.

Dearest Wilhelm,

Would it be a terrible nuisance if we stopped correspond-
ing for a few weeks? I'm planning a short holiday to Greece, I
really need it—

> handkerchiefs, towels, shorts, slippers
>> sponge, soap, toothbrush
>>> comb & brush
>>>> writing materials
>>>>> coca

Itea, Greece

23 April

In spite of the roaring spring heat I've been mentally lively
from the moment I set foot on Greek soil. Every hill, every
stone, every stream reminds me of classical motifs, and I have
found myself with a single leap hurled across a hundred generations into the glittering age of Greek knighthood. *Please* let this
be the place where, amid the endless pageant of the buried
past, I can finally find the secret of the ancient creative life.

I disembarked at Itea late yesterday afternoon. It resembled
a peninsula nipped off while red hot and allowed to cool into
an arm of lava. There were no hotels, so I found lodging with
two elderly spinsters, then this morning I met a miller with a
donkey who offered to take me northeast to Delphi.

Heading out of town along the Gulf of Corinth, we passed
valley after valley where hillsides covered with cypresses and
poplars and olive trees sloped down to the road. I noticed every

pebble; I looked long, long at every tree as we passed it, but each seemed to shimmer until it lost its shape. I suspect one enters Greece as one might enter a dark crystal: the form of things becomes irregular, refracted. Mirages suddenly swallow things, and wherever one goes the trembling curtain of the atmosphere deceives. This much is clear: sunshine in Vienna is only an imitation, a kind of silver-gilt, in comparison with the genuine, solid, unalloyed stuff that's lavished here.

By midmorning the day was ringing with near unbearable heat. When we passed a sandy beach I yelled to the miller to stop, left my clothes in the donkey cart, and walked down to the water. The surface was utterly calm, only dulled here and there with a faint wind like breath on a mirror. In the distance, islands sundered the identical blues of sea and sky with a darker blue ruler-stroke. I looked down at my body. The sight of my skinny arms, of my shoulders, which even conscious efforts could not keep from slouching, filled me with despair. I crouched down; the sand was wonderful, smooth like tiny pearls. A delicious radiance enveloped me, my whole being brimmed to the surface of my skin. There was a clump of mint growing nearby, the perfume overpowering. I broke off a stalk, crushed its leaves, rubbed them all over my body. I looked down at my muscles without shame, with sudden joy; I judged myself not yet strong, but capable of strength—harmonious, sensuous, almost beautiful.

I waded into the water, let my eyes wander in the wide watery expanse, let my gaze glide away and dissolve in the monotonous haze of the wonderful emptiness. I felt a longing for the unarticulated and the immeasurable—for eternity, for nothingness. Perhaps now I could slip underneath the unbreakable, inescapable spell that had held my mind and senses captive and be transformed into a new being—a demigod whose blood was water, whose hair was grass, whose eyesight was sunlight, whose breath was wind, whose thoughts were clouds.

I dived beneath the surface into the most ancient of homecomings; a large black boulder materialized, so I grasped it with my hands and launched myself down into the endless light. The sea floor rose and fell, grew closer, then farther away through water so blue with depth it glowed toward twilight. There were multicolored sea creatures, orange iridescent sponges, translucent purple starfish studded with glistening frail antennae. I was fully suspended, without rise or fall, no down, no up, north and south nothing; then, as wonderfully as I had descended, I began to soar, spewed up on a rising billow, ascending evenly with incredible velocity until I felt my body shoot up out of the sea like a flying fish. Colors, sounds opened out; the moment opened; everything opened with a flutter of gulls. A wild joy, an unbelievable feeling of hilarity, shook me convulsively from the depths of my heart.

Back on shore, I rejoined the miller. In an hour or so Delphi village was rising before us, terrace on terrace bleached in the midafternoon sun, the houses built up into slim tiers with narrow alleys and colonnades running between them, red, yellow, umber, and a jumble of pastel shades which the light transformed into a dazzling white city built for a wedding cake.

I paid the miller and found the village square; there, under a plane tree next to the well, some men were sitting as though they had grown there, immobile, not speaking to each other. I nodded to them and sat down on a low stone wall. I was not so much tired as intoxicated, dazzled.

There was a barber shop across the square. My hands went to my beard; for the first time in years it bothered me. It seemed ugly, artificial—a useless garment I could now safely strip off. I hated looking like what I had been: a medical student, a bookworm. I needed to express outwardly the inner change of my being; it was essential that nothing should interfere with my rebirth.

I entered the shop and sat in the marble chair. Neither the dubious razor nor the yellowing brush nor the smell could make me waver. The barber himself was of mythological quality, imposing with his mane of hair and his manner of moving as if he wore a heavy cloak. When he shaved me, I felt he was peeling off a mask. Afterward, in the mirror, I found my features quite handsome. I resembled a hard-grained peasant, one with a natural nobility about him, neighborly, industrious, with honest eyes, worthy of his great ancestors.

I said to the barber, "Isn't there a fruit tree around here someplace?" I spoke in Homeric Greek.

"Each tree bears its own fruit," he replied. "And each grows according to the ground where it sinks its roots."

"But isn't there one tree whose fruit is a joy beyond all?"

"Every joy is beyond all others. The fruit we are eating is always the best fruit of all."

I paid and left and saw what had eluded me before. Above my head, above the village, above everything—beyond my power of reckoning distance—loomed the massive flank of Parnassus, splendidly visible through a thick wreath of turbulent red cloud. It seemed an impenetrable boundary cast up at the edge of Earth. Worship this mountain? Yes, one could do that.

Hitching my bag, I left the square and climbed through the streets, lifting my gaze from the rooftops to the sky above— from the ephemeral to the eternal, from death to life, from man to divinity. Was that snow up there, or was it a trick of the light?

Three great hawks swooped by. The past and future coalesced and sought to envelop my approach.

Fifteen

After a while, following a steep path up the crest of a hillock, I saw a large white house set like a die on some flat rocks already venerable with the scars of wind and rain. Wearing a long full skirt of some colorful material, Sophia stood in the door with her arm raised in welcome; behind her long cool stare there was something wild and taunting.

I ran to her and seized her hands. "In vain have I struggled, Sophia. It will not do. My feelings will not be repressed. You must allow me to tell you how ardently I admire and love you!"

"Ah, don't make love to me! Too many people have done that," she said, frowning.

I took a step backward: it was the bitterest rebuke she

could have given me. But she seemed to relent and spoke rather more warmly. "Sigmund, you great clamorous baby-detective. You're obsessed with sex and completely ignorant of nature. What's happened to your beard?"

"I . . . wanted . . ." The words wouldn't come; I could only gaze at her without moving.

"Come in, Sigmund. I've been expecting you all day." She took my hand and led me into the drawing room, lovely and gracious with its whitewashed walls and bright paintings and books. "Have you eaten anything? Would you like some wine?"

I made not the slightest motion, but merely continued to gaze at her—at the slightly too large lips, which stand out vividly from the olive face; at the magnificent nose, delicately chiseled; at the eyes, which are in some way challenging but nonetheless seem to be asking for forgiveness.

"I'm not sure what to say, Sophia. I needed to get free . . ."

She poured me a glass of wine. "The capacity to get free is nothing; the capacity to *be* free, that is the task."

Handing me my glass, she sat composedly down, and after a moment I sat opposite her. The silence that followed seemed to lay on us with the weight of things final and irrevocable, seemed to crush us down like our gravestones. In all the wide future I could see nothing that would ever lift the load.

"Look," I said finally. "I admit I have many defects, as a physician and as a man; but there is such a thing as pure accident, you know, and the consequences do not attach to one. People are free. Nothing's done that can't be undone."

She threw me a glance of such exultant sarcasm that it

required no partner in its pleasure. "A man can live by accident and die by accident, Sigmund."

"I loved you, you know," I brought out.

"Please don't—"

"Try to understand something, Sophia. The artist in me has been given the upper hand over the doctor. I'm a sort of a madman as well as a doctor—a hybrid creature."

"Is that why you hate people?"

"Perhaps. In every disposition there is, I believe, a certain defect, a natural defect that not even the best education, the best course of study, can overcome."

Lucy came into the room, and I saw at once why I had been summoned: she was pregnant.

I rose and stared at her. She was more beautiful than before. The childishness had gone. There was a new and severer radiance. From the top of her head to her sandaled feet she seemed bathed in life and beauty and well-being. Her limbs were smooth and rounded, lightly tanned by sun and wind. Her hair was fair almost to whiteness, sharp like splinters of light. Her body was full of southern energy. (I thought, momentarily amid a thousand other things, "How strong she grows. She'll be as strong as I am. She'll have that as well as beauty.")

"Well!" she said, exhaling with all the emphasis of wonder and welcome.

"How long have you known?" I asked her.

"Three months; since I've been here."

I had known it, without knowing it, all along. After the first minute or so there was no shock, little surprise. Quietly the fusion of past and present took place and everything fell into order, into the pattern she was obviously weaving for the express purpose of having the fruit fall into this monstrous Mediterranean peace at just the right moment.

"Have you wanted children, Lucy?" I felt I needed to say something. Besides, it seemed, to look at her, impossible; she was so young and far in spirit from any child-bearing.

"I get no feeling whatever from the thought of bearing children. I find myself completely outside of it . . . but I do have an intimation of something yet to come."

"And . . . the father?"

"I haven't thought about him—I've refrained." There was a delicacy, almost a floweriness, in all her form, but at the same time a certain attractive grossness. Pregnancy had accentuated all her honey-sweetness, all the rose-red and the ivory, the warm, breathing perfection of her. She even seemed (but that's impossible, I thought) taller than before.

(I see now that her true nature is not human but demonic. Her inner absorption is strange, almost rhapsodic. She has the body of an immortal demon disguised as a female child, a child with a rapt, triumphant look. She's a deadly rapt child with a strange unconscious bud of powerful womanhood.)

She looked at me in silence, then: "I don't like your eyes. You're planning some dreadful trick. Haven't I been punished enough?"

"I haven't come to punish you, Lucy!"

"But I must be punished, because I am guilty." She gave me a slow smile of secret complicity.

"Look here, Lucy." I glanced nervously at Sophia. "Let's settle this right now. Nobody is guilty of anything. I am not your father, of course, but I have a feeling of great tenderness for you. Along with Sophia, I am responsible for your welfare."

"Well," Sophia said a little bluntly as she rose and left the room, "you are the doctor, anyway, and one would like to know that mother and child are healthy."

I went to Lucy and took her hand. She recoiled in genuine alarm. "I only want you to examine me."

"You must believe me, Lucy; I want to help you."

"Help me!" Her childish petulance was charged with anger. "Sophia says doctors never help anyone and they'd kill a patient to verify one of their theories. Besides, I'm perfectly all right like this. Are you sure I'm suffering from hysteria?"

"I've no idea, Lucy. Let me examine you, then I'll see. I promise you I won't hypnotize you."

She considered this. "You won't hypnotize me? Or give me drugs? But that's all you know how to do."

"Yes—up till now I've done nothing else. But you must help me to think of something else. I was mistaken, Lucy, I know that. It's the method that wasn't good. With hypnotism the confrontation is too brutal. We must proceed gently, talk to each other, break down the defenses gradually. I missed you, you know . . ."

"Did you?" For a moment her face was keen and almost angry. "I thought you had stopped caring for me." A deep blush rose to her face and spread over her neck. "Wouldn't Sophia be absolutely mad if she found out we were lovers?"

"Good Lord, let's not talk that way."

"But we *are* lovers, aren't we?"

"Not that I know of."

A sort of white radiance of anger like summer lightning

ran over her and blotted out her blush. She looked at me long and hard.

"Lucy, I think I'm sick myself. I think I project my own sickness onto my patients, onto you."

"What sickness?"

"If I only knew." I hesitated. "What's certain is that I won't be able to understand my sickness until I understand yours. I must discover in you what I am, in myself what you are. Help me."

She was silent for so long that I crossed the room, then crossed it again. A sudden restlessness had possessed me, and I was tongue-tied by the sense that our minutes were numbered, that at any moment Sophia might return.

"It's a collaboration you're asking of me?" When she finally spoke, it was in a low voice that I had never heard. Her expression seemed to alternate between a look of confidence and diffidence and one of sensitive expectancy.

"Yes, Lucy."

"You want us to be cured together?"

"Yes. And by each other."

She was impressed and pleased. "Let me think about it. Begin the medical exam."

Mother and foetus are in perfect health.

I have come upstairs to sleep. My room is huge, airy; whitewashed walls, almost completely bare. The quietness alone makes this another country, another lifetime. The only company is rock, air, sky—all the elementals.

Sleep, in this cool, still room, is like entering a cave.

Sixteen

Delphi

24 April

After breakfast Sophia set out for her Calydonian dig. It was the calmest day—pure spring, quite hot, yet the sunlight on the ground, as Lucy and I relaxed in our chairs, looked young and gentle, not fierce like the summer heat.

"We might as well begin," I said. Everything seemed propitious: the profusion of flowers, the dazzling early sunshine, the space between my thoughts. The lemon tea I continuously drank seemed to blend with the scent of rose geranium, wisteria, the delicate new leaves, the breathing darkness of the spring earth.

"What do you want me to say?" she asked.

"You must have something to say to me, Lucy, for

Heaven's sake! Tell me what you like. This way we'll search together, and the nearer you get, the nearer I'll get."

"But what exactly shall we be doing?"

"Well . . . you'll talk about whatever you like."

"Like a parlor game?"

"Yes, like a parlor game. Now begin."

"What with?"

"With whatever you like."

"Just this first time, you could probably help me."

"Very well, Lucy. Did you have a dream last night?"

"Yes . . . I was looking for something—just seeing if I could wander away, wander forever and see strange and beautiful things, one after the other to the world's end . . . But it's no good telling someone your dreams! It's idiotic! It doesn't mean anything."

"On the contrary, it means a great deal. Tell me, Lucy, have you had this dream before?"

"Oh, yes . . . I think the sweetest thing in all my life has been this place where all the beauty comes from."

"And . . . your dream begins—how?"

"It begins . . . well, not like a dream, for I go into my room and without lying down or even sitting down find myself standing on the bank of a bright and great river. And on the far bank I see a flock—of sheep, I think, but with fleeces of such bright gold that I cannot look steadily at them. The air is as sweet as music, and there is a pool of very dark shadow, clear-edged, under every tree. I go into the river, into the cold water, up to my knees, up to my belly, up to my neck, and then lose the bottom and swim and find the bottom again and come up out of the river into a pasture. Ahead of me are two small but upright figures, two raggedly dressed little girls of perhaps ten and twelve, gazing at me from a distance. Both are tanned to a gypsy darkness, with immense black luminous eyes. I approach and discover they are called Anastasia and Antiope . . ."

"Continue."

"The three of us start to walk through open country; there are goats and sheep and other animals. After a while the surface of the earth starts to smoke with bright yellow dust; then the air grows cooler and the fierceness of the blaze that has beaten all day diminishes. We climb a hill. Soon we're gaining height at a vertiginous pace. Couples of eagles, patrician and aloof, circle and drift through their last flights of the day. To the left is a pale orange sky, but to the right the mountains and sky are darkening.

"We make a turn and see a dozen or more people milling about near the entrance to a cave. There are dogs and cats and donkeys tethered to trees and goats nibbling invisible vegetation among the rocks. A meal is being prepared—bronze caldrons of whey are bubbling over fires of thorns, dripping cloths full of wet cheese hang from branches amid haversacks and blankets. Anastasia, Antiope, and I are given wooden spoons and half-calabashes of warm milk sprinkled with salt. With a tilt of her wrist, Antiope empties her milk into the blur of a dusty bowl. The liquid falls in a great round moon; it expands to the edges, and shapes define themselves—crescents, a whole menagerie of rabbits, goats, sheep.

"Suddenly a donkey kicks up a cloud of dust and the last rays of the sun turn it into a transfiguring red-gold curtain. Through the curtain, the trees glow with the light they have been storing up since dawn . . . The light shines from inside them like slowly expiring lamps . . . I won't tell you anything more. I'm too tired." She spoke with utter weariness.

"Nonsense, Lucy. Continue."

She raised her head. "No, there's nothing more to be got out of me today. You've squeezed me like a lemon."

"Lucy"—I almost said "darling"—"there is a golden light in you that I wish you would give me."

She looked at me. "But I don't want to give you things. I want you to serve my spirit."

I forced a smile. "I know you do. I know you don't want to give me physical things by themselves. But I want you to give me that golden paradisal light that is in you . . . which you don't . . . Give it to me."

There was a moment's silence, and then she replied, "How can I, you don't love me! You only want your own ends! You don't want to serve *me*, yet you want me to serve *you*. It is so one-sided!"

I wanted to shut off from her; it felt as though I had been struggling for hours up the face of a steep precipice, and now, just as I had fought my way to the top, my hold had given way and I was pitching down headlong into darkness. Perhaps if I could have got her in my arms, I might have swept away her arguments; but she held me at a distance by something inscrutably aloof in her look and attitude, and by my own awed sense of her sincerity.

At length I began to plead again, for I had to press for the thing I wanted, the surrender of her spirit. "You say I don't want to serve you, but my kind of service is different from other people's. I can serve you in another way . . . not through yourself, somewhere else. But first we must be together, Lucy, without bothering about ourselves—be really together, because we are together . . . as if it were a phenomenon, not a thing we have to maintain by our own effort."

"No," she said, pondering. "You're just selfish. You never have any selfless feeling of enthusiasm, you never come out with any real spark toward me. You just want yourself, really, and your own affairs. And you just want me to be here to serve you."

"Well, Lucy, words make no matter. The thing is between us or it isn't. Nothing is yet spoken in its true form; this age of ours will one day be the distant past."

"You don't love me."

"I do, but I want . . ." For a moment I saw the golden light of spring transfused through her eyes. More than anything I wanted to be with her in her world of proud indifference, but I knew it must happen beyond the sound of words. It was ruinous to try to work her by words alone. Her soul was a paradisal bird that could never be netted. It must fly by itself to the heart.

"I always think I am going to be loved and served," she said, "and then I am let down. Why don't you want to serve me?"

A shiver of rage went over me at her repeated use of "serve." I said, irritated, "I don't want to serve you because there is nothing there to serve. What you want me to serve is nothing, mere nothing! It isn't even you, it's your mere female quality! And I don't give a straw for your female quality!"

"Oh! That's all you think of me, is it?" She rose. I flinched from the measureless rejection with which her face looked down upon me. "I know what you want. You want me to be your *thing*, never to criticize you or to have anything to say for myself."

"No, damn it. I want you to drop your assertive will, your frightened apprehensive self-insistence, *that* is what I want. I want you to trust yourself and me so that you can let yourself *go.*"

"Let myself *go*," she echoed in mockery. "I can let myself go easily enough. It is you who can't let yourself go, who hang on to yourself as if it were your only treasure. You—*you* are the Sunday school teacher, you *preacher . . .*"

I was silent; then: "There you are. While ever either of us insists to the other, it is all wrong. The accord doesn't come."

"It is your will," Lucy insisted. "It is your bullying will. You want to clutch things and have them in your power. Why?"

"Why do you think?" I felt the blood rush into my face.

"Sophia says you haven't got any real body, any dark sensual body of life. She says you have only your will, and your conceit of consciousness, and your lust for power."

She sat down. We stayed together in stillness in the shade. The day was white around us, but we were in the darkness, barely conscious.

29 April

The days here are endless. The very shadows seem nailed to the ground, as if the sun no longer moved.

Today again Lucy and I were all day alone upon our bare

promontory with its beautiful clean surface of metamorphic stone covered in cypress and olive and lemon. The rock face (in the shape of a *mons pubis*) splinters the light and reflects it upward and downward.

The distant gulf looks cold but blue as the grave while the sun is blazing.

2 May

Sophia off at her dig. The silence up here is like a discernible pulse, the heartbeat of time itself. Every curve is a caress, a nakedness to the delighted eyes, an endearment. (I shall probably have a breakdown of some sort if I stay any longer in this house under the strain of this intolerable temptation.)

4 May

Cloudy morning for a change; I loll.

The cotton trousers Sophia has given me are a pale lilac color. Wearing them with a white shirt, I am like one of those inflated pale spiders you see in old gardens, sitting in the middle of a luminous web, giving little jerks to this or that strand.

Right now my web is spread all over the house as I listen from my bed like a wily old spider. Is Lucy in her room? Is she performing her ablutions?

I am torn between thought and feeling, between silence and screaming the house down.

Midnight

I was in bed but couldn't sleep. I stood up, soaked my hands and face in water, then, pushing open the door to my balcony, stepped outside. Not a sound, not a breath; the very air seemed to be asleep. I climbed down and listened . . . To what? Nothing; everything. Each sound entranced me.

I walked on in a kind of ecstasy. I walked at random, without purpose, without constraint. My mind seemed numb; my blood was singing with an increase, a recrudescence of life; my veins felt the afflux of a richer, hotter blood, touching everything, penetrating everywhere, stirring and coloring the most remote, delicate, secret fibers of my being—

7 May

It was still enough to have dinner under the cypress trees in the light of a single candle. I felt an unmistakable hint of festivity in the air, enough to make me wonder whether Sophia might not have found something important at her archaeological dig. From time to time she took up a large curved conch shell that lay on the table, and without reference to anybody blew a shattering blast. It was a strange, rousing noise that made the heart pound.

Lucy wore a long flounced purplish skirt. She had heaped necklaces around her neck and put gold rings on her fingers (they had a wonderful glowing reddish color) until she shone with barbaric splendor. My awareness was keenly fixed on her brown arms and throat in the candlelight, on her brown toes in her sandals—I was aware of a hundred images at once and a hundred ways of dealing with them: the stars shining down bright and taut upon our pure Euclidian surface; the bowl of wildflowers on the table; the bucket and axe by the door. The English knives and forks. My restless cough as I reached for a glass of wine.

Over apricots and coffee Sophia broached the subject of her Calydonian cave, giving us wonderful hallucinatory descriptions of kneeling in the dark with her pocketknife and scraping at the ancient corpses.

"How many skeletons have you found altogether?" I asked her.

"Six. Four are largely decomposed—probably servants buried with their masters—but the other two, royal corpses, I believe, are intact, because someone bothered to put them between layers of pebbles and burn enough wood around them to consume the clothes and flesh as a purifying process. The process and the gold I've found point to a civilization of positively Minoan splendor."

"Fascinating. How did you proceed?"

"Well, I first turned my attention to the larger of the royal corpses. The breastplate was more than two feet long, of pure gold. That was marvelous enough, but what was hidden underneath was even more stunning—a perfectly preserved torso, and on top of it a face that was almost palpitatingly alive. I stared down at the closed eyelids, the broad, bald forehead, the vacant area where there had once been a short nose. The thin-lipped mouth disclosed a complete set of thirty-two white and perfect teeth. I moved on. The second corpse excited me even more. What a face! Youthful, oval, with a high forehead and a long Grecian nose, the hairs of the eyelashes and eyebrows being exquisitely marked. She filled the dark still beehive of her grave and spilled out into the open. She flooded the cave and the fields and mountain pastures beyond. She lifted the sky a little higher. I am sure she is a woman."

"I doubt it very much, Sophia," I said.

She brooded; then: "Why not? The *Iliad* says queens as well as kings were accompanied in death by priestly heralds. Why do you *consistently* devalue female sexuality?"

"I don't devalue female sexuality. On the contrary, I observe that the sexuality of girls often has a thoroughly masculine character. Males are often passive, females quite active, in their childish erotic ventures."

"Are men of one blood, Doctor?" It was Lucy; I had forgotten she was there.

"Of one blood? I'd be sorry to think so."

"Then how do you arrive at your theories of the past?" She spoke with downcast eyes and a face that was radiant but extraordinarily quiet.

"Well, Lucy, I'm struck by the fact that the world is full of men and women belonging to different centuries who have to live together and be contemporaries. So I look for a theory that accounts for their differences and instabilities and difficulties in understanding one another. You see, I believe we're all more or less imprisoned in our conventional emotions—ruled by their inertia. Our feelings are cruel precisely because they're inert. They lag a full lifetime or more behind our actual lives. They're less human, not more, than the society we live in."

"As a result?" she inquired. She seemed genuinely interested.

"As a result, Europe is peopled with creatures who live

only with a small fraction of their being in the time to which they belong, the age to which their years entitle them. The greatest part of them is somewhere else, perhaps on another star or in another century—or simply in their childhood, as I believe is the case with you." I hesitated. "Do you know the word 'incest,' Lucy?"

"Of course I do."

"Well, if ten doctors and scientists were asked to designate one universal institution, nine would likely name the incest prohibition; some have expressly named it as the only universal one. But I think we should consider the evidence for the opposite hypothesis—that it is incest itself, and not the absence of incest, that has been universal for most people in most places at most times. And if hysteria is induced by history, it seems to me the doctor's task in therapy parallels Sophia's uncovering of the Minoan-Mycenaean culture behind the Greek—or would, if we could ever get rid of our defenses of medical knowledge, culture, world visions, and disinterestedness."

Seventeen

Delphi

10 May

A vast lawless sky; not a cloud, not one wisp of haze.

Lucy and I sat on the rocks in the white pure sunshine. She was gazing intently at the landscape, her uptilted face thrown back almost at a right angle to the taut lines of her throat.

I slitted my eyes and looked at her searchingly through my eyelashes. After a while her angled face, sitting on the column of her neck like an irregular roof, was no longer a face but merely a continuation of her throat, an extension from the throat with possibly a far-off resemblance to the head of a serpent.

Slitting my eyes further, I let her features grow more and more indefinite until they touched the boundary at which they threatened to lose their human character and become no face at all. For a moment, instead of a face I saw a unity so strange, so powerful and feminine, that I was curiously reminded of something, some unresolved riddle that emerged from the sea of memory and transposed me into a mode beyond convention far back in childhood. (Dark was the cavern of her nose, white was her chin fluted out like a hill, like a miniature beard sprouted the hedge of her eyebrows. Beyond the clearing of the forehead, cut by finely ploughed furrows, appeared the edge of a blond forest which blended imperceptibly with the woodland verge of Sophia's lemon orchard.)

"Have you been dreaming, Lucy?"

She yawned. "The sun is so high that I have no shadow . . . I'm walking over burning sands carrying an empty bowl." Her voice was unmoved and sweet, like a bird singing on the branch above a hanged man.

"Continue, please."

"There are two men and two women and two donkeys. I ride one of the donkeys. The sky stretches farther into space than any sky I've ever seen. It's as though only an error in gravity pins me to my donkey's back, prevents me from being assumed into infinity. We enter a low stone courtyard; I dismount. The journey has swollen my feet. Stretched on a sack, I find it pleasant to feel the cool air on them, so that I find their pain almost agreeable. Dusk sweeps from the sky, piles itself up in the corners of the courtyard. The walls grow less distinct; everyone falls asleep. Only I am awake. I turn to the wall, but sleep will not come. I am not conscious of any fatigue. I think of the joy I am experiencing along with the pain. With how much greater self-confidence will I now refuse the ordinary things! How much more assured my outlook on life will be!

"The sky becomes lighter; soon the sun and moon are shining brightly together, illuminating the side of the courtyard where I lie. The women build a fire between three stones. We sit around a sort of stew in which everyone hunts for his portion with his fingers. Water from a goatskin—delicious. Afterward we climb a mountain that looms up in the pale morning light. Just light enough to see. Rough path. On the other side, the country is irregular but level—beds of small broken stones, gravel winding around the hollows. Is it afternoon here? Shadows cast by the rising moon cross swords with those of the setting sun. Hawklike birds hover and wheel in the air.

"Later, we stop. The moonlight is brilliant. I have never seen such a moon, so white, so blinding, so large. It illuminates our surroundings as clearly as if it were day. I spend an hour dressing my feet by the light of the moon. Poor feet that have managed to jump and run, how they hurt! I don't know where to put them so that I shall no longer feel them. Finally I stretch myself out, sandals under my head, and sleep, not soundly, but each time I awake I am less conscious of pain in my feet.

"In the middle of the night we start again. On our left are bare mountains of some size, surmounted by one whose rangy black summit stands out in the sky. Always I ride my donkey, even though I should prefer to walk. Why do they insist on my riding? Perhaps they want me to save my strength for later on? Well, I continue. That is my only objective, to keep going. One single thing to do, to arrive. I will sleep anywhere, suffer anything. Rocks, gorges, rough, somber mountains. It doesn't matter. I pass among them . . ."

She yawned, and it was enough to bring me back to consciousness that it was a human being and not a landscape I was regarding. For a minute I felt a mild discord, a rasping together of two worlds, like the two bits of a broken bone.

We sat on in the garden. The sun made its usual round of the house as the afternoon ripened into evening.

I had a glass of wine. And another. Warm dusk deepened into an amorphous (I almost wrote "amorous") darkness.

12 May
The days pass without incident in this huge and ancient stillness. I feel muted, unreal, my presence left out.

13 May
Until nightfall, I do not speak ten words. At dinner Sophia promises to take me to her "Minoan" cave.

14 May
We left for Calydon at dawn, tramping resolutely down toward the coast, Sophia singing a song called "Take Me to the Apple-Laden Land." The sky lay in a heroic blue arc as we

came down the god-haunted mountain. After an hour or so, I saw, looming up like a stage set, the remains of a crude stone altar thrown down and smashed to pieces (local earthquake?). I sniffed the air; it smelled strongly of burnt meat quenched with wine. A dim wisp of old smoke uncurled into the sapphire sky.

We moved on, continuing our descent. I began to smell the unmistakable smell of pine, rolling up to us like a fresh mountain stream. Soon we were in a sweet pine forest. Life became something quite new. I felt immensely happy. I embraced the trees, felt them breathing, felt the deep places beneath their roots, between their trembling branches. For the next few paces, it looked as if we were walking straight into the empty sky; then suddenly we were on the brow of a steep slope looking down. At the same moment the sun, which had disappeared in the pine forest, leapt out again, and it was like gazing into a new world.

There at our feet, cradled amid a vast confusion of warm blue lands, hills and forests far below us, lay a small valley as bright as a gem, a sort of cleft in the mountain's southern chin. There were thousands of wildflowers and wild vines, and many groves of flourishing trees, and a great plenitude of bright water—pools, streams, and little cataracts.

Slowly, we began descending. The air came up to us warmer and sweeter every minute. I could hear, down below, everything, the very chattering of the streams and the sound of bees.

"I'm quite sure this is the secret valley of Calydon," Sophia said. Her voice was hushed.

"It's secret enough," said I. The freshness and wetness all about were making me somewhat anxious. I more or less decided the valley was a dreadful place, full of the divine, sacred; no place for mortals. There might be a hundred things in it I could not see.

Sophia looked at me to steady me; I remained motionless under her gaze. After a minute she pointed to a sheer wall of dark rock like a theatrical backdrop, at the bottom of which was a cave of imposing size. "It's a little bit dangerous, so follow me, and be careful."

Inside it was rather cool but not damp. Striding forward out of the sun, Sophia lit a torch and stuck it into the wall. I caught my breath: brilliant frescoes leapt out at us with all the blues and reds of the Minoan-Mycenaean age. There were snakes and jewels, and cupbearers and sloe-eyed girls and tawny bulls tossing youthful riders. "Wait here," she said, stepping behind a ledge. I heard her move some rocks, then some time later she returned, holding a strange, twisted gold mask in the shape of a lion's head, which at first I took to be a helmet.

"Is it a death mask?" I asked. Death was certainly marked on it, though there was no hint of repose in the awesome features.

"Something rather more complicated, I think."

"You're being horribly smug, Sophia."

She carried her head high, like a pretty woman challenging a roomful of rivals. Her Turkish trousers seemed woven out of candle beams.

"Almost it is godlike, don't you think, Sigmund?"

"You mean—?"

She looked at me with dark interrogation. I searched her rapt face, the face of an almost demoniacal ecstatic. "I mean this mask is the image of Oeneus or some other king of Calydon at the moment of dissolution, when he became a god. The artist has grappled with death and depicted it with immense power and simplicity—yet no one knows the precise purpose served by these masks. Neither Homer nor any other Greek writer refers to death masks of any kind."

"What are you saying? What are those holes near the ears?"

"Deliberate perforations. The mask was wrapped around the face of the king by means of threads; then, when the metal heated up—"

"Heated up?"

"Gold is flame, at least to the early Greeks. Homer says the spirits of the dead will only be admitted to the realm of the dead after burning. Perhaps Patroclus on his funeral pyre wore gold as a raiment of flame." She seemed amused at the idea.

"This is the second mask." She held it out; I bowed over it. "Look at the benignity. The features are masculine, but not brutal. The thin lips are pursed in a mysterious smile. The large eyes are closed, the eyelids clearly marked. Look at the eyebrows—they're heavily incised and curl upward in imitation of the cheeks. The effect is to give an unmistakable feminine depth and curve to the face, as though it were seen magnified at the end of a long corridor, beckoning."

She returned the masks to their hiding place and brought out an oval gold plaque about the size of a belt buckle. On it were wondrously wrought figures. "Heinrich calls it the signet of the Mother Goddess. He hasn't seen it yet, of course, only some photographs. Look, the bare-breasted Earth Mother sits beneath a tree with flowers in her hair. Two women of noble aspect approach, probably priestesses, Artemis and Aphrodite for choice. Like the Mother Goddess, they're bare-breasted; like her, they wear flowers and ornaments in their hair."

"Who are the other figures?" There were two of them, one standing before the goddess, introducing the priestesses, the other climbing a small cairn of stones, plucking fruit from a tree and offering it to her mistress.

"Handmaidens."

"And what's that hieroglyphic?"

"I was wondering when you'd get to that," she said. "Above the scene, the sun shines in full splendor beside the cresent moon; it is at once noonday and the depth of night. If you ask me, this is the key to the quiet composure and serenity of everyone involved. There are no extraneous elements—no veils, no altars, no rituals—yet the power of the heavens flows down in rings of light. Artemis and Aphrodite come to the Mother as though by right, towering over her with none of the servitude one sees in Egyptian paintings of the same period. Even the handmaidens possess a very human dignity; bathed in the light of the sun and moon, they stand and move according to their own volition." Her voice had changed. Her whole tone and look were enveloping me in a soft inaccessibility. "We can never hope to fully understand the meaning of the signet. For instance, are those oranges or lemons hanging on the tree? Heinrich thinks they're breadfruit, such as he's seen in South America, but I strongly disagree. And what meaning can we attach to the six strange objects that decorate the left side of the signet opposite the tree—are they masks, sacred flowers, lions' heads, or merely decorations to balance the tree with its heavy fruit? Heinrich says the waving lines beneath the sun and moon represent the ocean, but to me it is far more likely they represent rings of heavenly light, or the Milky Way, or Mother Earth with her uneven surface of land and her rippling sea."

Her eyes were black, velvety. The pupils glowed like onyx, by turns forsaken and probing, and on them there seemed to float a curious iridescence, a sort of film of disintegration and sullenness, like oil on water. A spirit of recklessness entered me. Perhaps it was only that my hands sought some object to hold to absorb the sudden energy coursing through them; at any rate, I took her shoulders in a firm grasp and said, "If we don't do this now it will be worse afterward—worse for everyone."

She turned her head away. "There are still some things one doesn't do in broad daylight, aren't there?" She wrestled free and moved to the back of the cave (perhaps 150 feet). I followed her meekly. I hated it. It grew darker at every step. It was the first time I had ever visited a cave, but it convinced me that I didn't like them.

When we had gone as far as seemed possible, she said, "This is where it begins to be difficult. Follow me closely, close enough to touch me at all times, and don't lose your nerve."

She stepped behind an outcropping of rock and scrambled into a hole about four feet above the cave floor. I followed, very much alarmed, but too craven to beg off. It was just possible to move on hands and knees. I crept after her. I couldn't see anything, but I could tell when, after a dozen yards or so of a creeping progress over rough stone, we began a horrible descent. I had to brake strongly with my arms. The hole grew smaller. Sophia never spoke or called to me, but at one point she seemed to drop from her knees and crawl on her belly, so I did the same. I was as frightened as I have ever been in my life, but there was nothing for it but to follow, because I had no idea of how I could retreat.

My shoulders and neck ached torturingly. I had not wriggled on my belly since I was a child, and it hurt. At every hunch downward my stomach, groin, and knees scraped mercilessly on the stone floor. At last Sophia said, "Here we are," and as I crawled out of the hole and stood up—very gingerly, because the darkness was all but complete and I had no idea how high the roof might be—there came a flame from the torch she had lit.

Slowly, in the flickering light, the inner cave revealed itself. It was about the size of a modest drawing room; it might have held fifty people. It was very high, for the roof was above the reach of the light from the torch.

"I discovered this inner cave about a month ago." Sophia spoke in a low tone. She was becoming soft, subtly infusing herself into my bones, as if she were passing into me in a black electric flow. She was in a mood I had never seen in her before; all her irony and amusement were gone, and her eyes were wide with awe. She said, "The outer cave was known to several people, but nobody seems to have noticed this inner one. I believe I am the first person to enter it in a thousand years. And you are the second." I said nothing. I couldn't bear the thought that a barrier of words might drop between us. Without words we had a strange electric comprehension in the darkness. Her being suffused my veins; I felt the electricity turgid and voluptuously rich in my limbs; it seemed to concentrate at the base of my scrotum, like a fearful source of power. She walked toward the farthest wall, and I followed. We came to a small enclosure formed by a barrier of heaped-up stones.

Above the barrier, carved into the cave wall, were seven niches, seven little cupboards. In the uncertain light, I could just make out something of bone in each of them, old, dark brown pieces of bone, which I gradually realized were the skulls of animals.

"Bears," said Sophia. "Look how bones have been pushed into the eyeholes. Here the leg bones have been carefully piled under the chin of the skull."

"Did bears . . . live in here?" I felt incapable of thinking two thoughts in sequence; my brain seemed to whir, undone, in my skull.

"No cave bear could come through that passage. *People* brought these bones here and set up this place of worship. Our ancestors worshipped bears. Perhaps someone pulled on a bearskin and there was a ceremony of killing. There are such caves as this all over Europe and Asia. They've even found some in America."

"Does it matter . . . now?"

"Yes, it matters now. What do we worship today?"

"Is this the place or the time to go into that, Sophia?"

"Where better? Look around you. We share the mysteries with these bones. We stand now where men and women came to terms with death and mortality and continuance. How long ago, do you suppose?"

"I haven't any idea."

"It was certainly not less than fifteen thousand years ago—possibly much, much more. Look at me, Sigmund. Doesn't this place give you any sense of the greatness and indomitability and spiritual splendor of man? Are you too much Apollo—"

"Sophia, don't. We mustn't quarrel. Not here. Let's get

out, and I'll argue all you please. But for the love of God, let's get back to the light!"

To my astonishment she flung herself on the ground, face down before the skulls, and remained there for perhaps three minutes. When she arose she was grinning. "Back to the light, my child of light. You must be reborn into the sun you love so much. Let us lose no time."

It took forever. What had been horrible going in, because it was done head downward, was less horrible but more difficult coming out. I had to wriggle upward at an angle that seemed never less than forty-five degrees. Out of the darkness into the gloom, out of the gloom into the sunshine, renewed and reborn by the terror and mystery and immemorial age of the cave.

Eighteen

Woke feeling absolutely new; marvelous; to breakfast very hungry. Lucy was alone at table, looking detached, beautiful, and more than ever pregnant.

I thought, is she better or worse than in Vienna? Perhaps neither. Perhaps she has completely failed to understand the reality of what is happening to her; perhaps for her, pregnancy is merely another dream among many come to life; perhaps that explains her peculiar attitude—she perceives all this experience as merely a more intense form of dreaming. Something in her expects to wake up and find everything ordinary again; that's why she's so heedless of her surroundings. (Yet surely I am dreaming, too?)

"Are you plotting something, Lucy?" When she looked at me, I thought I had never seen anything so beautiful.

"Once I have completed this dream, my youth will be over. I shall enter on another life."

"You mean adulthood?"

She paused, then answered with sudden resolution. "My head is full of a single expression of will—to bring it to an end, to reach my goal . . ." (She was silent for so long that I almost spoke.) "On my donkey I look at my hands; they are almost black with gold veins. A woman's voice speaks of a cavern where a river flows. I feel joy. There are multiple golden forces transfiguring me, uniting me by one will, one power, transforming me . . ."

"Where are you going, Lucy?"

"I know now that it is my father who must be reached. He alone, as he writes his name in the earth, can give weight and final shape to my poetic purification, bring it out of the formless to the formed. My tastes are simple; let me have the sun as I am. I will be like a rider in the mountain passes, trusting myself to my donkey—a little pressure on the reins, perhaps, a little steering, but done wisely.

"Dawn; the sun rises slowly because we are following the valleys. We change direction, and instead of traveling east move toward the south, crossing some hills which gradually increase in size, their contours resembling various animals. Birds with heavy wings cry as they soar overhead. It starts to rain; it rains heavily. We reach a lake and drink. Always, always we keep going.

"Night, and moon. I am given a handful of pomegranate seeds. The juice spurts into my throat; to the last moment it is good. It leaves a pleasant tartness, which lasts for a long time. The seeds are of a pale rose at one end, changing imperceptibly to a clear pure white, a color as fresh as the juice is good.

"I wait for sunrise. It happens gradually, like a golden wave spreading over the earth, leaving small islands of shadow here and there. Then the moon reappears, the sun sinks slowly, and darkness spreads over the earth. I feel an unspeakable fatigue. I want desperately to sleep but cannot. The small of my back is aching.

"After a while, the sun rises again, radiating a rosy glow in every direction. Gradually I discern a dark outline straight ahead—the outline of an olive tree, isolated. I want to rest my eyes on it for a long time, I want to let its molten stream flow in me, putting an end to thought. But soon the rosy glow fades, the olive tree passes, and the sun, continuing to rise, brings other shadows, puts another face upon the earth. I do not know where to put my back and shoulders. I am drying up completely. Something is close, a presence, very near—"

There was a crash of broken china: she had crushed her cup to pieces in her convulsive grasp. Shards were falling at her feet, thick black coffee was seeping into the earth. Blood was crimsoning the tablecloth. She had cut her finger to the bone. I took her hand and put it in my water goblet. "Lucy, Lucy." She was horribly pale, as pale as a girl on her deathbed. Finally I succeeded in stanching her wound with an application of cigar ashes; I lifted her into my arms and carried her indoors. It was dark in the house after the sunlight. Like sleepwalkers we ascended the stairs, which creaked under our feet. We crossed the dark landing. I couldn't quite see her face; it seemed to be flowing away from me, flowing between the banks of her hair, so I brushed my lips against her skin to assure myself that it was there. I found her forehead, her eyelids; I found the curve of her cheeks, the line of the mouth.

In her room there was a cloud of white lace enveloping the bed and washing-table. Of course! This was the central point of the house, the hidden altar round which all the other rooms were built. Lucy slipped from my grasp and walked toward the bed. I followed confidently, my hand touching the brass rail, moving over to the blanket beyond, from wool sliding over to the smoothness of the turned-back sheet. I got in; I could hear her sobbing inhalation of breath. A spring creaked faintly. I was already hard. Quickly I got on my knees and straddled her from above. My knees pressed her temples. Sweat burst from my forehead. I unbuttoned myself and pushed in between her lips. Flaming red daggers danced before my eyes. My orgasm was horrible, draining. I wished that it would go on forever, would increase a thousandfold and annihilate me utterly. No sex had ever made me feel like this; I had assaulted her, yet she had subdued me.

I got out of bed and listened. Silence. Was Sophia in the house? It didn't really matter. I needed to take breath in some other world, even if only for a moment. Something awful was happening to me; an enormous reservoir of despair was overflowing in my veins.

Outdoors the air was electric. I felt the blood rush into my face. Without thinking, I took the upward path. Somewhere away on my left I could hear a faint hum, a sort of smothered, rumbling noise that seemed to be caused by golden chimes. There was a light film of debris, broken branches and rocks, over everything—why? I climbed for an hour or so before no-

ticing a black cloud on the horizon like a chariot. It mounted
the sky and quickly obliterated the sun. Then a great flash laid
the world bare to my eyes. It thundered as if the sky broke in
two, straight above my head. Bolts of lightning, one following
the other, pricked the place where I stood, left, right, near and
far, everywhere. And each flash showed falling trees; they
seemed to fall silently, for the thunder hid their crashing. But
there was another noise it could not hide; the walls of Parnassus itself were breaking. I saw or thought I saw fragments of
rock hurled about and striking on other rocks and rising into
the air again like a child's ball that bounces. Then there came,
as it were, a flash of lightning that endured; that is, the look of
it was the look of lightning—pale, dazzling, without warmth
or comfort, showing each smallest thing with fierce distinctness—but it did not go away.

I blinked my eyes and looked down at my feet. There was a
stream in front of me. I hesitated, then stepped into it. The
water rose so quickly that I was overtaken by its rush before I
could stumble back from it, wet to my middle. Birds started
flying irregularly through the air, shrieking. I was affected with
a fearful nausea.

Suddenly the ground beneath my feet opened in huge
trenches. Frightful, hideous caverns yawned on every side of
me—

"Lucy!"

She was a foreshortened figure far below, clinging to the
trunk of a golden tree whose branches lashed the ground, a
divine object not transposed but of the earth, an apple tree
alive in its exposed cone of lava, with beautiful golden fruit and
sunlight gliding in and out among the leaves—silver on top,

gold on the bottom, bronze along the twigs and stems, and metal-black and gold on the shadowed trunk. The ground swayed violently. I found myself tumbling through the air, and when I found my feet again, I was standing next to her. She looked at me, her stare level and unafraid, her feet apart, arms hanging at her sides. Never had I seen a face so calm and so unearthly. She pulled my hand to the shadowed trunk, forcing my fingers into the dark metallic bark. "Touch it. Beat your head against it." Something hateful and strange had begun. As if I could thrust it back by brute force, I fell upon her in anger. Before I knew what I was doing, I had her by the shoulders and was shaking her as one shakes a child. At the same time I felt an approaching release, a fountain of life rising up in me. Soon we were wrestling rapturously, like lovers, two essential small figures working into a tighter, closer oneness of struggle. Her reciprocation was marvelous!

A contraction clamped her middle and I realized what was going on: she was in labor. I made her comfortable, as far as possible, on the ground.

It was a long, harsh struggle. As the lightning-like light softened and the sun reappeared, the child was born, lifeless.

A shiver of horror passed over me. My face, heated with my exertions, suddenly chilled. I turned my attention to Lucy, who lay collapsed, almost pulseless. I worked feverishly to revive her; after a few minutes of effort her heart strengthened and I turned back to the child. A girl, perfectly formed. The limp warm body was white and soft as tallow. The head lolled on the thin neck. The limbs seemed boneless. The whiteness meant only one thing: asphyxia pallida.

I laid the child on the earth and began the method of

respiration, rubbing her with leaves, crushing and releasing the little chest with both my hands, trying to get breath into that limp body. Time passed. Sweat was running into my eyes, blinding me, but though my own breath came pantingly, no breath came from the lax body of the child.

"It's stillborn," whimpered Lucy.

A desperate sense of defeat pressed down upon me, a raging hopelessness. All dashed away now. Futile, beyond remedy. I felt a longing for the child so overwhelming that I dropped her, wet and slippery, next to Lucy, like a strange white fish.

I covered my face with my hands and broke into the hottest tears I had ever shed.

Nineteen

Hotel d'Angleterre, Athens
19 May

Sometime afterward I became separated from Lucy. I have not seen her since.

Descending the steep paths that detrude the southern flank of Parnassus, I had the impression of wading through phantom seas of blood. Arriving at the level of Sophia's house, I was amazed to find it had survived intact—though the great rocks, if possible, looked more parched and convulsed than before.

Inside all was deserted. There was an ample supply of food and water, and plenty to read, though I had no desire to look at a book. In my room I found a note from Sophia: "We're going to Iliou Melathron. See you there."

Finally this morning, after four days, a goatherd appeared

and guided me down into the clear bright workaday world of Delphi village. There I hired a conveyance with some difficulty, and I arrived in Athens after nightfall. It is windless in Athens. After a meal at the hotel I am looking down on the large square, Syntagma Square, which seems black with people, thousands of them, seated at little tables loaded with drinks and ices. The waiters scurry back and forth with trays to the cafés adjoining the square.

20 May

I presented myself at Iliou Melathron ("Palace of Troy"), Heinrich Schliemann's mansion on Panepistimiou Street, to be told that Mrs. Schliemann was at her mother's house in Colonos, an hour or so away. In the Schliemann carriage, bowling along on the outskirts of Athens, I remembered that Sophocles had been born in Colonos and had immortalized the place in Antigone's words:

> Father, poor tired Oedipus, the towers
> That crown Athens still seem far away.
> As for this place, it is clearly a holy one,
> Shady with vines and olive trees and laurel;
> Snug in their wings within, the nightingales
> Make a sweet music.

Modern Colonos turned out to be a tree-shaded suburb of modest though pleasant country villas. The coachman set me down, and I walked up a path obscured by a profusion of honeysuckle, jasmine, and ivy. A short, plump woman appeared in answer to my knock. She smiled and led me around the side of the house to some chairs under the trees. *"Kathiste."* I sat down. She turned and went back around to the front of the house. At the same time, Sophia came out of the back door, carrying a large silver tray. She came forward, nodded to me, set down the tray, and sat down.

It was cool in the garden. There were climbing vines with grapes and several varieties of fruit trees—pomegranate, almond, apricot—and a muskmelon with spongelike yellow flowers. On Sophia's tray were two glasses of water, a silver cup with two silver spoons, and a glass bowl filled with cherries in a thick red sugary syrup.

Neither of us spoke. I stared at her slashing black eyebrows. For a second our eyes met; then she cast her eyes down and with a graceful little movement of her hand chose one of the spoons, plunged it into the bowl, dug up a spoonful of cherries, and swallowed it. She held her empty spoon over one of the glasses to catch in the water whatever syrup dripped down, then drank the water, put the spoon in her now empty glass, and returned the glass to the tray.

I imitated her actions in every detail. When I had finished, she spoke. "It's called the ritual of the sweet spoon. The purpose is to break the ice."

"Where's Lucy?"

"In a place where you can't find her."

"Do you know, Sophia, I believe I've redefined myth as a result of my trip to Greece—'Myth is the human imitation of actions near or at the conceivable limits of desire.' "

"Ah, my poor Sigmund—I suppose this had to be. But

congratulations are in order, no? You have successfully intuited the intimate, passionate relation between classical mythology and human fantasy."

"But?" I almost screamed at her. "But?"

"But surely mythology is far more than an aid to scientific analysis."

"I don't understand you, Sophia. You haven't yet explained things for me."

"Myths aren't explanations, Sigmund; they're stories that project us into participation with the phenomena they tell about, so that the need for explanation falls away. Think of Homer, the blind man who saw the Greek islands in the flaming light of his imagination."

"Homer was a poet."

"Homer was half a poet and half an adventurer who created and dwelled in a higher spiritual world in which the objects of perception in this one had become transfigured and charged with a new intensity of symbolism."

"Perhaps Homer was mad."

"Was it madness to believe that a very bright and wonderfully pure civilization had once existed and that it was worthwhile to enter that civilization, even at the risk of lunacy?"

"Enter it why? For what reason?"

"To find oneself, to regain what is one's own. The goal of reason and courage has always been the regaining of identity, and this goal is embodied in literature as it was once and still is embodied in mythology."

"You can compare—"

"Why not? Naturally a displacement occurs when gods in myths become heroes and heroines in books, translated downward to suit new conditions of authorship and readership. But we don't have time today to probe the mystery of the emergence of literature from mythology. The point is that no poet, no artist of any art, has his meaning alone. When someone asked Blake, 'When the sun rises, do you not see a round disk of fire somewhat like a guinea?' he answered, 'Oh no, no. I see an innumerable company of the heavenly host crying, "Holy, Holy, Holy is the Lord God Almighty!" ' "

"Could Blake exist in modern Vienna?"

"Why not? Just like us, he could see the guinea-sun whenever he wanted to—it was a common example of a sensation assimilated to a general, impersonal, abstract idea. But when he saw the angels he was not seeing more *in* the sun but more *of* it. He was the first person in the modern world to see the events of his day in their mythical and imaginative context. Unfortunately, our century is busily translating the speech of the poets into the language of psychology, psychopathology, psychosis. What on earth is the use of all this separation and isolation of phenomena through observation and description, this incessant separation and dismemberment of people into diagnostic categories and classifications? Myths cannot be told in exclusively rational language. If psychology wants mythology, it needs a new way of scientific description, a new language inspired by prophecy and visions as well as science, a language that can change the structure of consciousness, male and female, spirit and body, logical and mythic.

"I don't mean to lecture, Sigmund. But I do want to align myself with Blake and the poets. I reject the rationalistic vocabulary of the common man—the consensus upon which in our time the peace of the Augustans has been arranged and maintained. But I can see that you are scandalized. Oh, well. I had hoped to enlist you as a messenger into the world, but you fear, perhaps rightly, that your work might be scientifically drained, reduced to mere literature. Never mind, Sigmund. Would you like more cherries?"

Twenty

5 Maria Theresienstrasse
23 June

Hail, cherished Wilhelm!

I have left you unconscionably long without a letter, but I
want to tell you about my Greek trip, which I took in a
grumpy mood, but from which I returned refreshed. It was
indeed pleasant to walk in bright sunshine among the whitewashed houses of Athens, to see the trees covered with orange
blossoms, eat candied fruits, etc. The splendor of the ruins was
comforting in the midst of the poverty of modern times.

But now I can't wait another minute before confiding in
you something that happened to me toward the end of my trip.
Outside her marble mansion near the royal palace, by purest
chance, I ran into Sophia Schliemann with Lucy O—and Lucy

was calmly developing a nervous pregnancy, and it was *I* whom she thought she was pregnant by!

But perhaps this will not surprise you? In which case merely throw the following hypothesis into the wastepaper basket: in every instance, repression starts from the feminine aspect and is directed against the male one; that is, "impossible" loves such as Lucy's for her doctor have their origin in the fundamental masochism of the feminine. What do you think? It's incomplete, I know. But I believe the foundation is right, and it is perhaps something that can cement your work to mine, place my structure on your base. I'll write it all down for the sake of our common work. As always suggestions, amplifications, refutations, and explanations will be received most gratefully. Obviously, the establishment of some link to the general biological and anatomical aspects of bisexuality would be invaluable.

Meanwhile, my friend, the world is full of wild things— stupid ones as well (the latter, however, usually are people). For two weeks I have had an influenza with fever, pus, and cardiac symptoms. It has shattered my well-being! I rarely have felt so low and down. Some earlier work on anatomy is proceeding more or less, but so what? All my interests have lost their meaning, my practice is especially poor, and then I am, as far as my mood is concerned, mostly useless. Today at least I can write. But am I really the same person who was overflowing with ideas as long as you were within reach? Now when I sit down at my desk in the evening, I often do not know what I should work on.

But perhaps it is not so important how I was and how I am. Just now, writing to you, I am my old self again, vigorous of heart, and wild, and yearning to enjoy some of the coming weather. Write to me soon with your marvelous ideas and findings. I do look forward to seeing you, to hearing what you are up to and rekindling my almost extinguished energy and scientific interests from yours. What I need now is work that's clear, precise, rigorous, objective. No more dream gold for a while! Anatomy, histology, physiology—therein lies my salvation. Hypnotism was interesting, but it doesn't cure. It's not a therapy, it's a cabaret turn.

I can hear you saying, "Never rely on the mind. Always confirm your ideas through experiment. The biological development of the individual invariably takes place under the control and direction of the sexual organs."

Do you remember the Helmholtz creed, Wilhelm? "The living organism is part of the physical world; it is made up of systems of atoms moved by attractive and repulsive forces, following the principle of conservation of energy."

Your faithful
Sigm. Freud

POSTSCRIPT

20 Maresfield Gardens
12 September 1939

My physician, Max, was here again this morning (he is analytically trained as well as being an excellent internist). I coughed, inhaled, and held my breath according to his direction. It cost me an enormous effort. I can't bear to have to do everything with three times the effort others use when I was accustomed to doing things more easily than they.

"Max," I said to him, "do you remember how you used to pooh-pooh the idea of the alchemists that gold had medicinal value? I notice your fine scorn does not prevent you from using alternate doses of the salts and the filings of this metal. You use concentrated arseniate of gold against anemia, muriate against syphilis, cyanide against amenorrhea and scrofula, and chloride of sodium against ailments like mine."

Did he hear the irony in my words, I wonder? Does it matter? I have no illusions. My judges will regard all this as grist for their mills. *Au fond, ça m'est bien égal.* What science and irony had to offer was a lifeless, rationalistic way of looking at things; what came from their mouths was a dead philological language of no help to an understanding of the spirit, the psyche, put it as you please. Who had a longing for *that* had to stand alone, the only living creature in the hot silence of the Mediterranean midday, among the relics of the past, and look, but not with bodily eyes, and listen, but not with physical ears.

In Arcadia, everything begins over again at its commencement every instant, each fraction of an object is as laden with meaning as the cosmos itself. There golden apples overcome everything with phallic-narcissistic bravado. Indeed, why not? The capacity to imagine something that is absent and symbolize it in representable form appears early in human life; most children under the age of ten believe in amulets, sacred fountains, votive offerings—in a force superior to life and in the need to place oneself under the protection of that force.

The gods dazzle our eyes. They flow in and out of one another like eddies on a river, and nothing that is said clearly can be said truly about them. Holy places are dark places. When Lucy entered my life (where everything came late, money and fame), it was the return of the repressed, for the most vivid, long-buried memory of my early years was of my mother drying her long chestnut hair in the sun. To dry the underneath hairs she would throw them over her face, and I would be left with a ball of hair with golden glints in it. Gold became the screen that concealed yet symbolically revealed my deepest fear and desire—my own disappearance. (*Naturam expelles furca, tamen usque recurret.* "You may drive out Nature with a pitchfork, but she will always return.")

What a relief to see my mother's face again! Even with its secrets and vows, its standards of impossible perfection, its tears, kisses, gondolas in the moonlight. Oh, how is the gold become dim! How is the finest gold changed! I would give my life to see Lucy again for an instant by my bed and to touch her hand. If only she were here I could lay my head in her lap and cry like a child—

Suddenly she is there before me, holding out her hands for me to take. The air that comes from her clothes and limbs and hair is wild and sweet. Youth itself seems to come into my breast as I breathe it; surely I have come to the highest, to the utmost fullness of being that the human soul can contain.

But now, from a strange look in her face or from a deep doubtful quaking and surmise in my own heart, I know all this has been only a preparation. Some far greater matter is upon us. The air is growing brighter and brighter. Something has set it on fire. Each breath I draw lets into me new terror, joy, overpowering sweetness. I am pierced through with the arrows of it. I am being unmade. I am no one.

Author's Note

There is some confusion among Sigmund Freud's earliest cases as to which represents the first full-length, or reasonably full-length, analysis of a case of hysteria using hypnosis in cathartic therapy. The chronology as it stands is self-contradictory. Even James Strachey, Freud's original English translator, speaks of "an inconsistency in the accepted account of some of Freud's activities after his return from Paris in the spring of 1886."

It is probable that as a precaution against betraying some of his early patients' identities, Freud altered the times of their treatments and failed to carry the changes through consistently in his records. This suggests a further possibility, namely, that Freud altered the place of residence of some of his patients. There are tantalizing hints that a trip he took to an estate in Livonia in 1891 may have happened earlier and in a quite different part of Europe, possibly a resort.

Two things are certain:

(1) that Freud's oft-repeated claim that his external life was devoid of drama is disingenuous.

(2) that the whole problem must remain, in Strachey's words, an "open one."

Acknowledgments

I would like to thank my father and mother, James Michalos and Claire Michalos, for their ideas, assistance, and encouragement. Thanks also to Jesse Cohen and Nan Talese, to Elizabeth Racine for saying "Go," and to Craig Jones for saying "Freud."

About the Author

Of Greek descent, Peter Michalos grew up in Iowa and New York. He attended Yale University and studied filmmaking at the New York University School of the Arts. After working as a copywriter in an advertising agency, he went free-lance, writing and producing television commercials, industrial shows, and various corporate events. He also traveled extensively in Greece and the eastern Mediterranean, and it was on the Aegean isle of Spetsai that he started work on what eventually became *Psyche*. Peter Michalos lives in New York City, where he is working on his next novel.